The Girl Who Was Silver

Danger on the Other Side

The Girl Who Was Silver

Danger on the Other Side

David Gerrold

Star Traveler Press

ISBN-13: 979-8-9925058-9-4

The Girl Who Was Silver copyright © 2025 by David Gerrold
Editor and Publisher: Justin T. O'Conor Sloane
Cover art: *Silver Girl* © 2025 by Bob Eggleton
Book design by Katerina Bruno

Published by Star Traveler Press
an imprint of Starship Sloane Publishing Company, Inc.
Austin-Round Rock Metro, Texas, USA

starshipsloane.com

Printed in the United States of America & internationally

CONTENTS

FOREWORD

In a 2015 interview for *Lightspeed: Science Fiction and Fantasy* magazine, author David Gerrold explained of science fiction literature:

> *When I was nine, science fiction was an amazing discovery—it was an escape from a world I didn't understand into one that was far more interesting [...] But you got to hang out (metaphorically) with Heinlein, Clarke, Asimov, Leinster, Andre Norton, and the many others who were reinventing the universe. There was a sense of inevitability that these were genuine reflections of what the world would be someday. I was impatient to get there.*

Many science fiction readers and writers experience the feeling that they've been born slightly out of their correct time period, that the world isn't as it should be, or certainly not as it is in their mind's eye, that they have been born ahead of their time, or that they have a strong vision (almost a waking dream) of a different, alternate world. However, it is only particular science fiction writers like the "Big Three" of Isaac Asimov, Arthur C. Clarke and Robert Heinlein who write with sufficient expression and power to share their sense of vision compellingly. To that list of writers, we might also add the name David Gerrold.

Gerrold wrote one of the best known and loved episodes of *Star Trek: The Original Series* —"The Trouble with Tribbles". If you've not seen the episode recently, it contains all the essential ingredients that produce a "classic" episode: socio-political themes, a deceptive alien species, a moral problem to be resolved, escalating jeopardy and, most importantly, humour/love of the most human type. It is precisely these elements, but particularly the latter, which typify all of Gerrold's works, from his Hugo and Nebula Award-winning novelette *The Martian Child*, to his numerous science fiction and fantasy movie and TV scripts, to his several dozen novels, novellas and collections, to his countless contributions to the wider genre and community.

The novella we present here, *The Girl Who Was Silver*, is no exception, naturally. Indeed, it is a moving work with more "heart" than you'll find in many a science fiction. Moreover, it is arguably as progressive and visionary as any of Gerrold's work, with its refreshing consideration of new types of human relationship, alongside a concern for the loss of all privacy in our cyber-society. And it's got marauding trolls to boot!

Like Isaac Asimov and Arthur C. Clarke, Gerrold worked closely with Gene Roddenberry on the *Star Trek* shows, bringing us a very human vision for the new era in space travel. We should always remember that such a vision often turns out to be more than mere fiction—instead, it becomes future fact, the vision guiding our way towards the new reality. The line between future fiction and fact is perhaps more blurred than we sometimes realise or like to think.

Arthur C. Clarke's *Exploration of the Moon* was used by Wernher von Braun to convince President John F. Kennedy that our moon was reachable, that journey then visualised with a new realism by Clarke and Kubrick in *2001: A Space Odyssey*. Isaac Asimov famously brought us/invented the words and concepts of 'robotics' (in his *Robot* series), 'positronics' (as per the Data character's positronic brain in *Star Trek: The Next Generation*) and 'psychohistory' (in his *Foundation* series); he was then Special Science Consultant on *Star Trek: The Motion Picture*, a movie which brought the new realism to the *Star Trek* franchise, anticipating both the Voyager VI space probe and the dual wonder-and-threat of A.I.

Yet, were it not for writers like David Gerrold, the new realism and our future reality would probably have a lot less heart to them. Hear once more the yearning and excitement in his words from the interview:

There was a sense of inevitability that these were genuine reflections of what the world would be someday. I was impatient to get there.

Then enjoy *The Girl Who Was Silver*!

—A J Dalton (Dr Adam Dalton-West)
November 2024, London, UK

ONE

Silverlight hair. Porcelain skin.

Eyes the color of the evening sky, a gaze as pale as ancient ice.

An immortal.

She made no effort to hide her disease, slipping through the crowd as silent as smoke. She'd look the same a thousand years after the rest of us were dust. If she chose.

She must have been searching for something, or someone. She wouldn't have come down without a reason. Here in the dirt we lesser beings liked to pretend we understood the immortals, liked to pretend we knew their pain, could see past their dispassionate stare. Some of us even thought we could speak to them as equals. I suppose that amused them, watching children dance and prance and occasionally beg for elevation. A fool's game. I turned away, put my back to her, returned to my drink and thoughts of darkness.

It didn't work. She found me anyway. She

slid into the place opposite me. She smelled of something I couldn't identify, sweet but musty. Time and darkness and something else. Her gaze was inescapable and uncomfortable. I glanced away. The rest of the patrons of the club pretended not to notice us. I looked back to her.

"Mandarin," she said.

I shook my head. "No."

"Yes." She reached across and touched my hand. "You are."

I pulled my hand away. "What do you want?"

"You were offered a gift. You turned it down."

"If you say so."

"I was there."

"So why are you here now? I know the rules. 'Once refused the gift can never be offered again.'"

"I'm not here to offer anything. But I'm still curious why you said no."

I avoided her gaze. "Long story."

"I have time."

"I don't."

She nodded. "Your choice." She considered her nails, a deliberate gesture. Immortals never do anything by accident. Something in the change makes them think differently. Short-timers are impulsive and emotional. Those on the long ride think slower, more methodically. That's as near as I've ever been able to explain it.

She studied me thoughtfully. "Do you have

anything better to do?"

"I'm waiting for rigor mortis to set in," I said.

"We all are," she replied. "Some of us wait longer than others. What do you intend to do while you're waiting?"

I lifted my drink in mock salute to her. "This."

"Would you like a job?"

"Not particularly."

"Yes, I know. You don't need the money. Do you want the challenge?"

I shrugged. "I stopped looking for challenges a long time ago."

"No, it wasn't a long time," she said. "Maybe to you. Not to us."

"Still not interested."

"All right," she said. She gathered herself as if to leave.

"What kind of a job?"

She stopped herself so gracefully, her entire shift in posture had to have been planned. She knew even before she moved that I would have to ask and she would have to stop and turn back to me.

"Will you come with me?"

"Tell me here."

"I was sent to find you, not tell you."

"So you don't know?"

She didn't answer that. "Are you coming or not?"

What the hell. I followed her out, knowing

that behind my back every pair of eyes in the club were tracking our path. And the moment after we slipped out the door, the level of conversation would escalate from whispered to frenzied, from hungry curiosity to desperate speculation. It was the pattern. So what.

A dark limo waited at the curb. The doors slid open as we approached. She took the rear-facing seat, she pointed me to the seat opposite. I settled in without comment. There was a time I would have thought her beautiful, now I saw her beauty as unnatural and unnerving. It is possible to be too perfect.

The car slid through the night, a black shark cutting through a sea of darkness. She studied the view outside her window, the silent lights of the huddling city. Perhaps she cared, probably not. Finally she noticed me again.

"We're going up the hill," she said. "Not all the way up, but far enough. Farther than you've ever been. You are going to meet a man. You have never met him before, but he knows who you are and he is expecting you. You will have a conversation. At the end of that conversation, you will come back down the hill. There is nothing for you to say or do or decide. All you have to do is listen. Is that clear?"

Nodded. "*Esta claro.*"

"*Bien.*"

The car growled into the canyon and began winding its way up toward the summit. We passed through several visible checkpoints without being stopped and probably just as many invisible ones. We passed ranks of ostentatious villas, places where elite short-timers might mingle with immortals, but those quickly gave way to unremarkable gardens and parks, buffer zones. The road narrowed and darkened beneath a canopy of leaves. The headlights of the limo illuminated the sheltered groves. A few more curves and we turned into a slim drive that led up and around and finally onto a broad hilltop that overlooked the entire city, a matrix of light spread from here to the horizon. The city glittered, but its inhabitants were invisible. It could have been deserted, abandoned with the lights left burning.

We arrived at a curving path, wide, paved in stones that glowed a pale blue. The path led up a gentle slope toward a gazebo, maybe a temple, a delicate confection. A roof that floated above high slender pillars. Long white drapes drifting like smoke. An open fire-pit in the center. Graceful couches scattered around. The place was meant to impress with its casual elegance. Others would have been impressed, but that's because others still believed.

The door slid open and I climbed out of the car. She didn't follow. I looked back to her. She shook her head. "This is as far as I go."

The car door closed. The limo rolled away.

I shook my head, annoyed, and made my way to the fire pit. Blue flames curled softly around a bed of ice-colored crystals, but they radiated no heat. I passed my hand through the illusion, satisfying myself.

"You're not the first to do that."

I turned around. The man was short, but stocky. Red hair, ruddy complexion and heavily muscled, he was built for fighting. He didn't walk, he stumped. "Do you play chess?"

"Sometimes."

He spoke as if we were old friends just having a chat. "You play on an eight-by-eight board. Sixty-four squares. If you are serious, you can consider each move for an hour or longer. It's not a game of war as many people like to think. It's a game of relationships. It's a game of positioning. And on a board of sixty-four squares, the game is so complicated that you can spend your entire life studying the complex web of relationships." He spread his arms out wide. "I play on a board that has one thousand and twenty-four squares to a side. One million, forty-eight thousand, five hundred and seventy-six squares in all. Sixty-four different kinds of pieces and ways to move. I play as part of a team. Five of us. Sometimes we consider the relationships on the board for as long as a year before we finally move a piece. We play for position. We expect to be playing for position for a very long time. Long even for us. We do not expect the game to end before the universe dies. But we play it anyway. Multiple kings and queens. Thousands of pawns. Occasionally, a wizard or a knight.

Some pieces die of old age, others regenerate. Some never die. Would you like to be a knight?"

He held up a hand before I could speak. "No, stop. Don't answer yet. Would you like something to drink? Food perhaps?" He started to gesture toward an invisible servant. "What can I offer you?"

"I'm good. Some water would be nice."

"Of course." He finished the gesture, then waved toward a couch. "Please sit, Mandarin. Take off your coat. Relax. Chat with me a while. Unless you have something more important?"

"No, there's nothing." I sat on the opposite end of the couch. "You haven't told me your name."

"You may call me Red." He smiled. "For obvious reasons."

"How old are you?" Not always the politest question to ask of an immortal, but I'm not famous for my manners.

"Three hundred and seven years."

"You don't look a day over three hundred."

"Thank you," he said, absolutely unamused.

"Sorry," I said.

"No need," he replied. "I know it seems that immortals have no sense of humor. That's not true. It's just that after a few hundred years, we've heard all the jokes. All of them. Long before the hundredth repetition, all jokes become banal."

"So if you don't laugh at comedy, what do you laugh at?"

"Tragedy. Isn't it obvious? Tragedy and comedy are the same thing. Comedy is when it happens to someone else." He smiled. "I could tell you an immortal joke. You wouldn't get it."

"Try me."

"An old man owns a fine mare. This is good luck. The mare runs away. This is bad luck. The mare comes back with a fine stallion as her mate. This is good luck. The stallion is wild. This is bad luck. The old man has a strong son who is good with horses. This is good luck. But when the son tries to tame the wild stallion, he falls and breaks his leg; he is crippled for life. This is bad luck. All the young men in the town are conscripted into the king's army, but not the young man because he is crippled. This is good luck."

"And?"

"There is no 'and.' The old man is lucky, yes? His life is full of luck."

"You're right," I said. "I don't get it."

We waited while a servant delivered a tray with a pitcher of water and two crystal goblets. I assumed the servant was male, hard to tell. He wore a pale singlet and sandals and he had long silken hair that veiled his face, but the way he carried himself, his physique and his posture, he seemed like a boy of sixteen. I studied him while he filled the goblets, trying to estimate his age, or if I had guessed wrong about his gender. Like every other immortal, he was a distant cipher.

When I turned back to Red, his eyes were focused deeply on me. "You find him attractive?"

I shook my head—not a denial of the attraction, a denial of the question. I took the offered chalice and drank slowly. The water was cold, but not the cold of ice. It was another way to avoid Red's probing gaze. When I replaced the glass, Red was still waiting my reply. "Yes. He's very pretty," I admitted. A noncommittal answer.

"If you want him, say so," Red said, then added, "No, not like that. Although I suppose that might be possible too. He asked to serve you tonight."

I looked to the boy again. "Thank you," I said. The boy nodded without speaking, then removed himself to a courteous distance, beside a discreet service table. He could see us if we needed him. I suspected he could hear us as well. Trust nothing—it's good advice, especially in the clouds.

I turned back to Red, still drinking from his own glass. He allowed himself a smile. "Yes, we drink water. We eat food too. We have all the normal human functions. If you cut us, we bleed. We heal faster but we do bleed. We copulate, often very enthusiastically but just as often not at all. Sometimes we breed, not often but sometimes. We urinate, we defecate, we sleep. Occasionally, we even fart. We are immortal, but we are not immune. We are sensitive to direct sunlight, but it doesn't kill us. And you already knew this."

"Yes."

His expression changed. "We have a job for you."

Shook my head. "No thanks. I don't work for

Silvers. I thought you knew that."

"Your job is to spend some time here. That's all. We are paying you for that. We've already forwarded the money to your account." Before I could say no, he stopped me. "Take it, Mandarin. You need it."

I considered my options. I didn't have any. What was I going to do—walk down the hill? "All right. I'm here. And after I'm through here, then what?"

"Then you'll go home."

"And that's all?"

"Your cooperation would be useful, but it's not essential."

"Silvers always have a reason. There's more to this than just being here."

"Yes. Three years ago. We offered you the opportunity. You turned it down."

"And you want to know why?"

"I already know. Do you?"

I wasn't going to go there. "Let's just say I've seen what the transformation does to people. I don't want it."

"And what if you're wrong?"

"There's only one way to find out, isn't there?"

"Yes."

"That's why my answer is no. The transformation will change how I think. I'll end up thinking like you that it was worth it."

"Do you think we haven't examined this

question? Every single one of us. It's part of the transition. I can tell you this, Mandarin—most of us prefer our lives this way. And those few who do not . . . ? Yes, it happens. From time to time."

"Unfortunately, there's only one way out."

Red shrugged. "It's one of the parts of life. Ephemerals are terrified of it. Immortals have time. Your language doesn't have the right words to explain. Let's just say that Silverlights have a different relationship with time and death."

"See? That's my point. You think differently."

He nodded. "We have a different conversation, yes. But let me ask you. This thing that you think you are—what if there were something else? Something beyond your ability to experience or comprehend in your current condition?"

I didn't respond to that. Just as he had probably spoken this conversation a thousand times, I had probably heard it at least a hundred. The immortals were not the only ones who pondered the nature of their transition.

He looked at me dispassionately, "Can you really say that your current state is the best you can be?"

"I don't know about best. It's who I am."

"Who you are, Mandarin, is an illusion of belief," he said. "You are a construct of language trying to explain itself."

I considered his statement, then shook it away as meaningless, another incomprehensible riddle. An old man had a fine mare. His life was full

11

of luck.

"And you're what?"

"I am a conversation," Red replied. "Nothing more. I'm an illusion that knows it's an illusion."

"And you're asking me to be the same?"

"Is your current life so wonderful? We offered you a different possibility. The offer is still on the table. If you accept it, yes. If not, thank you for listening."

I nodded. "How long do I have to think about it?"

Red shook his head. "You've already made up your mind."

"You think so?"

"You think I don't know? I'm three hundred and seven years old. After a long enough time there are no secrets. Chess stops being a mystery. The interest is not in the game but in the positions the pieces choose to play. An hour ago, you were a rock, a piece that sits on the board and does nothing at all. It takes up space. But it always contains the possibility of becoming something else. Unless it decides to stay a rock. Are you happy being a rock? I don't think so. I think you've been a rock long enough. I think you're ready to be something else."

"And you think this will make me happy?"

"I don't know if it will make you happy. I know it will make you different. Do you want to be different? Or do you want to stay the same? If you stay the same, you know who you'll be for the rest of your life. If you choose to be different, you will never know who you are from one moment to the next, unless you invent it."

"I've heard all this before."

"You didn't understand it then. You don't understand it now. You won't understand it until afterward."

I considered my fingernails, wondered what my hands would look like if I became as pale as the wind. "You assume I'm going to change my mind . . . ?"

"I assume nothing. I have no need to assume."

"So why do you need me?"

Red's eyes were deep. Like a parent. "The truth, Mandarin? We don't. You're convenient, but we don't need you. Not in the truest sense of the word *need*. We can use you, that's all."

"Well, you're wasting your time."

"No, Mandarin. It's your time. Not mine, I have more than enough. You're wasting *your* time. Look in the mirror. Is this who you want to be? A self-righteous ass who takes pride in being bitter, self-centered, self-important, arrogant, and judgmental? You've let yourself get beaten up and beaten down, so many times that you've locked yourself away inside a shell of 'I don't care,' all nice and neatly closed off where no one can beat you again. And you have the gall to think that's some kind of integrity. It's not. It's selfishness of the worst kind. You contribute nothing to anyone and nothing to yourself. You use up oxygen. You suck the energy out of life and walk around in its dead husk. Do I need to say more or are you ready to see yourself in this mirror?"

I looked away, I looked back. I met his gaze. I blinked.

"Yes," he said. "That one."

"Fuck you." And for good measure, "Eat shit and linger."

"Right. Keep it to yourself. Nurture it like a cancer. Let it fester in your soul. It's yours and no one else's. Where's the payoff in that?"

"What do you know about it—" I stopped in mid-sentence.

"After three hundred and seven years, probably more than you. But if you want to be the expert on self-abuse . . ." He trailed off meaningfully.

I didn't answer.

"How long are you going to sit with it?"

I wasn't finished glowering.

"Come on, Mandarin. Who hurt you?"

"You already know the answer to that—"

"Do *you?*"

"Of course, I do—"

"Say it!" he commanded.

"Okay, yes, you're right. I'm an asshole. And no, I wasn't always."

His voice softened. "Go on."

"And yes, I know who hurt me."

"Say it."

"I did. I did it to myself. There. Are you

happy? I can be just as zen as you."

"Show me."

Took a breath. Another. A long deep one. I studied the floor. Pale blue stones, almost translucent. I wondered where they came from, how they were made, why they glowed. "Yes. Once I was young and foolish and enthusiastic. Once, I had a lover. And yes, I thought my life was finally complete. Stupid me. It was an impossible moment. The kind that you can't talk about."

"Why?"

"Because—because you can't. It's beyond words."

"Everything is words," Red said. "Everything is a conversation. Everything. When you get that, when you *truly* get that—"

"What? Life becomes wonderful?"

"No. Life is what it is. And you are what you speak. What you choose to say is who you choose to become."

I rolled my eyes.

"Or what you choose *not* to say." Red continued so softly I had to strain to hear him. "Do you think that what you had was so special that no one else can understand? Do you really think we don't know? That I don't know?"

My throat hurt. "You're right. I don't think about other people." I shrugged. "And they don't think about me. That's as fair as life ever gets."

Red didn't reply. He just studied me, waiting.

I took a breath. "I don't talk about it because

it's mine. It may be the only thing that is."

Red nodded. "If you say so." He motioned to the boy to bring us more water. We both waited until he returned to his post.

"So . . ." Red began. "What you're talking about is both infatuation and astonishment. It's such an unfamiliar and maybe once-in-a-lifetime experience for most ephemerals that the joyous wonder of it leaves you breathless. It's a moment—a realization, staggering in its immensity, of finally being part of something so completely human and unique and special that you can never be the same again afterward. And yes, sometimes there is sex, but not always. And if there is, it's only a physical expression of what's really happening—a synergistic collision of mind and soul and body, a transformation of the self into an entity that is both oneself and larger than oneself—an epiphany of recognition of two beings functioning as one for just that single sparkling instant of time." He looked across at me. "Correct? Is that what you're talking about?"

"You've analyzed all the joy out of it."

"All right. Let me speak it in your language. The summer sky is as golden as a dream and everything sparkles like champagne. You look into your lover's eyes and you see the face of God—" Again he looked to me with a questioning expression.

I didn't answer.

"And then—just as quickly as you found each other, you lost each other, it was over. Death separated you."

"Not death," I said. "Something worse." I put my chalice down. "And if you knew all this, then why do we have to have this conversation?"

"Because this is an employment interview."

That stopped me.

Finally. "I already said I wasn't interested."

"If you weren't, you wouldn't be here. You wouldn't have gotten in the car."

"I was curious."

"Really?"

"Why would an immortal need a short-timer?"

"We don't. We need a set of skills. We need someone who can go where we cannot."

I thought about that. Where could a non go that an immortal could not? Bright daylight was the immediate answer, but probably not the only one.

"So why pick me? You know who I am. You know how I feel—"

"That's precisely the reason. We know who you are. We know how you feel. Everybody does."

"Right." I reconstructed the phrase, "Bitter, self-centered, self-important—"

"—arrogant and judgmental," he finished. "Selfish."

"Bitter? Yes. Wouldn't you be? You talked about the golden moment sparkling like champagne. I'll never have that moment again. Never. That's why I turned away the gift of your disease when it was offered. I don't want to live the rest of my life without my other half. But that's the life I'm condemned to live. So I'll live it until the day it ends. You invite me to live this life forever? Why would I or any sane and rational person choose to live in festering despair for a thousand years or longer instead of only a few score? Why?"

Red nodded his agreement. "A very logical conversation. Thank you for your honesty." He paused, considering his next words. "I can answer your question, but I won't. It's your question. It's your responsibility to answer it."

"If I could answer it, don't you think I would have answered it already? There is no answer."

"I agree, there is no answer—not inside the conversation you choose to have." He smiled, but it was not a friendly smile. "You'll have to find a different conversation."

"I don't understand."

"Of course not." He glanced at the sky. The eastern horizon betrayed the slightest hint of a glow. "I need to speak with my colleagues. Laz will make you comfortable." He gestured to the Silver boy.

I followed Laz up the blue path. The garden was bigger than I'd thought. Each turn of the walk revealed more and more of the grounds. Here and there, scattered benches, pools, fountains, and other gathering places. If there was an order to it I couldn't tell, but I was certain there was. A satellite view would tell me nothing. The Silvers had a way of *changing* what they didn't want others to see.

Common suspicion had it that most of the keep was hidden below ground. The castle, the part that showed, was as much decoy as it was decoration. It was there to impress, a place to meet and gather. A charade for the servants to maintain, a facade to demonstrate the presence of godlings. Nothing more. So people believed.

True or not, the real world of the immortals remained hidden and secret, deeply removed from the knowledge of lesser beings. The Silvers kept themselves apart, only occasionally dipping into the realms of the mundane.

Laz, the boy—I assumed he was a boy, he could have been anything, an androgyne, a neuter, a trans, a cipher—led me to a seclusion, a place sheltered by a grove of towering trees. At some point, we were no longer outside, I hadn't noticed the shift, but now we were *inside*, beneath a roof without walls, held aloft by glass and illusion.

"If you have needs," he said, "just speak aloud. You will be heard. Food, drink, a bath . . . ?" He eyed my clothes. "A change of clothing, perhaps?"

"Are you—?"

"No. Not yet," he answered.

"Is it something you want?"

"I have no experience of the alternative."

"I see." Interesting. Something new to consider.

"Is there anything else you require?" Was

19

there something in his expression? I couldn't tell.

I looked around. White chairs and benches, a small fountain feeding a bathing pool. A white table. "I think I'm good."

Laz nodded and faded into the night.

I went to the table. A platter of fruit. A pitcher of cold water and several goblets. A clue? Was someone due to join me soon? I didn't trust the fruit. The water seemed harmless. I poured, I drank, I looked around. I sat on the bench and considered the conversation with Red. So I was just another piece on the board. I could be replaced. Obvious enough. We are the ephemerals. The downsiders. Short-timers. Flickers in the darkness.

So . . . why me? Why not any of the others? There was no shortage. And many who were smarter. What did I have that would justify the offer? Self-awareness? Not even that. What I had was . . . nothing.

Was that it? Was that the qualification? A person who has nothing to lose and nothing to live for? A person who has renounced all feeling? An empty vessel to be filled? An interesting insight. The gift is only given to those who don't want it.

There was something I was missing. That was the thing about the Silvers. There was always something else, something underneath.

A figure came out of the darkness. Her.

"It's getting early. Shouldn't you be heading toward your coffin?"

"Don't believe everything you believe," she

said. She sat down at the other end of the bench.

I didn't answer. Common wisdom about them. Don't talk. Wait. They're patient. Methodical. They will tell you only what they want you to know. So anything you say just gets in the way. No problem here. I had nothing to say.

She shifted her position so she could face me. Her expression was detached. Like all of them.

"I know you think you're being patient. You're not. It's a performance. You are impatient as the rest. It's because you have so little time. You have to move before you finish thinking."

I waited anyway.

"A long view is more useful than a short one," she said. "But sometimes circumstances demand immediate action." She brushed her Silver hair away from her lethal eyes, a deliberate gesture. "One of ours was murdered last night."

"I hadn't heard."

"We haven't told anyone. We don't want ephemerals knowing that we're vulnerable."

"You just told me."

"The others have decided. You're going to take the job."

"Don't I get a choice in the matter?"

She shook her head. "You chose when you got in the car." Her hair sparkled with the glow of the dawn. "The rest has been . . . the dance you do."

I shrugged. "All right. I'm curious."

She raised a hand to stop me. Her gaze was suddenly sharp and penetrating. "I can see the blood rushing beneath your skin. I can hear the beating of your heart. I can smell the secretions of your glands. I can feel your emotions as physical responses. I see you in ways that you cannot comprehend. I can assimilate all of this data as an immediate experience of who you are and what you're thinking. I understand the thought processes racing through your mind. You are . . . what you are." She did not complete the rest of that thought aloud. "You don't trust yourself because you don't trust your own kind. You don't trust us at all. But you respect us because you respect power."

"I don't think trust is the right word."

"It isn't. But you don't have the right word. Trust is the closest one." She pointed away down the hillside, toward the still-glimmering lights. There were fewer now. "There is someone out there who knows we can be hurt. Not one of us. Whoever it is, they have dangerous knowledge. They can expose us to greater danger. We need to find that one quickly. Before they can share that information. Before there are more than one."

"And—?"

"And we need to find that person quickly. We need someone who can investigate. Someone who will not be suspected."

"So you came downside and plucked me out of a crowded bar? That's not inconspicuous. I'll be the subject of gossip for weeks. Everything I do will be watched. Everyone I talk to will know. I'll have a spotlight on my every action."

"That's right. And when you go back un-changed everyone will know that you walked away from us. Again. That will be part of the gossip too. And the stories will spread, magnified by time and distance, about how much you hate us. And if the story spreads far enough, as we expect it will, then the person who hates us enough to murder one of us will seek you out."

"So all I have to do is go back down the hill."

"Yes, that's all. You're bait. So even if you do not take the job, you have already taken the job."

"Clever."

"On short notice, it will do. It draws more at-tention to our existence than we prefer, but we can use the distraction to cover many things. Other things besides this. Not your concern."

"And when the murderer seeks me out—?"

"You'll want to be careful."

"And . . . ?"

"And you'll do what you do."

"And that's all you want from me? Nothing else."

"That's all we can expect from you."

Time to change the subject. "You want some water?" I picked up the glass and crossed to the table.

"Yes, thank you."

I poured for both of us. "You haven't an-swered the question."

"You haven't asked it."

"Okay, I'll try again." I handed her a full glass. "Why me?"

"Because you're you."

I thought about my next words for a long moment. "Three years ago, you offered me Silverlight? For the same reason? Because I'm me?"

"Yes." The slightest hint of a smile.

"It doesn't make sense."

"It doesn't have to make sense to you. It makes sense to us." She drank. She put the glass down.

I put my own glass down. "Then I guess we're done here?"

"Yes, we are." She lifted a shoulder—perhaps a graceful shrug of dismissal, but the movement suggested a whole encyclopedia of meaning. She stood. "The car is waiting for you. Whenever you're ready." And then she whispered away. The sun was already large in the east.

Down the hill. The limo dropped me off at my battered old car. I was too tired to be embarrassed. I poured myself in and told the pilot, "Take me home." I put the seat back and fell asleep.

TWO

I **was looking into an oven,** the pizza wasn't ready and I needed to pee. Where was the toilet? The oven door banged—

Woke up in the carport, my back aching, daylight streaming in at me—well, that explained the oven. Something was banging on the car, bouncing it like an empty oil barrel. I struggled to sit. "Up, dammit." The seat did its bending thing and lifted me upright. Strange dreams. No, not a dream. Blinking painfully, I rubbed my eyes, wondering where the hell—

"Oh." And then, "Shut up!" to the troll pounding on the roof of the car, punching a few more dents into its battered hull. Poured myself out onto the pavement, staggered upright, red-eyed in the morning blare. "What?! Can't a guy sleep in his car when he wants?"

It rumbled at me. "Boss wants you."

"Forget it. I'm not off life-support before

noon."

"It's after."

"Even worse. Where's coffee? I need to pee."

Trolls do not understand much. Coffee is one of the things they do not. Peeing is another. This one had an unkempt pelt—unkempt even for a troll—and smelled like two-day old garbage. He yanked me by the neck and dragged me to the troll van, threw me in the back like a sack of trash. The van groaned and sagged as he climbed in after me. "Station," he rumbled and the van lurched forward.

Despite the pain shooting through the various parts of my body, or maybe because of it, I felt strangely aware of my surroundings. I wondered if there had been something in the water last night. I still needed to pee.

We arrived. The troll pulled me out of the van, dragged me through the corridors of the station, dropped me on the floor outside the boss's office. "I need to pee," I said.

"Boss wants you."

"Does the boss want to see me pee?" I pushed past the troll toward the restroom. The troll blinked in confusion. Maybe it knew enough not to follow. Who knows what trolls think?

I staggered into a stall and peed for a long satisfying time—long enough and hard enough to get an uncomfortable pee-shudder. But it was relief—enough that I could now hear the complaints of my empty stomach. I splashed water in my face, ran fingers through my hair, straightened myself up as much as possible, and reentered the world of daylight and pain.

The troll grabbed my shoulder and pushed me into the boss's office.

"Geezis, Mandarin! Don't you ever change clothes?" She sniffed and made a face. "Or take a bath for that matter? You smell worse than a troll."

I sagged into a chair. "I love you too, Mom."

"Don't call me that. What did the Silvers say to you last night?"

"More of the same. Nothing useful."

"I'll decide that."

"You got any coffee?"

She gestured at someone behind me. I didn't bother to look. "A donut would be nice too."

"Don't press your luck."

An officer put a mug of black coffee on the desk in front of me. And two donuts on a plate. The coffee smelled life-threatening. The donuts looked stale. But it was better than nothing.

"There are fifteen Silvers up the hill. And maybe twice that many acolytes. Which ones did you see?"

"Her. And a man named Red. And a service-boy named Laz." I took my first sip of the coffee, made a face. "No one else."

"Eat or drink anything?"

"Only a couple glasses of water." Thought about it. "That might be why I skipped the usual hangover."

"Or you slept through it. It's already three." She frowned. Her usual expression was a frown, so she didn't have far to go. "What else?"

"The usual existential tautology. And chess. And why I'm such an asshole."

"And?"

"And why did I refuse the offer?"

"What'd you tell him?"

"The usual. I don't want to glow in the dark. It'll be too hard to fall asleep."

"Old joke. Very tired. Now what are you not telling me?"

"They had a job for me."

"For you. A job."

"That's what they said."

"And you said?"

"I said I don't work for Silvers."

Mom thought about that. She's not my mom. She's not anybody's mom. But everybody calls her mom. I never bothered to ask why.

"What else, Mandarin?"

I shrugged. Drank some coffee. Cool enough to drink. Still awful tasting. I wondered why I wasn't sharing the part about being bait. If I did that, the word would get out, there are no secrets in the basin, and that whole gambit would implode. I'd be done. So why was I keeping silent? Curiosity about the murder? More than that. I wanted to know who could kill a Silver. And how.

"We know they transferred a large sum of money into your account last night."

"They said they were paying for my time."

"That's all?"

"They don't explain a lot. You know that. They do what they do."

"And you do what you do. And you don't explain a lot either."

"I'm retired. I don't have to explain anything."

"You still have a license." Mom chewed a fingernail. "You want to keep it?"

"The only thing I can give you is this. I think someone took a stick and stirred the ant hill."

"Why do you say that?"

"Because after Red and I talked, he said he had to speak to the others. Then they sent me home."

"So let's see if I understand this. They took you up the hill, talked about nothing in particular, offered you a job—which you refused—and then sent you home again."

Another swig of awful coffee. "Yep." I wondered if I could trust the donut.

"There's something you're not telling me."

"I haven't told you my underwear size." A deflection.

It didn't work. "36. You used to be a 34 until 32 months ago. That's also when you went from tighty-whities to boxers." She wasn't guessing.

I hesitated. I already knew the police were monitoring my financial transactions, but until this moment, I hadn't known just how deep. The unnerving part—that Mom was tracking such personal information *and* remembering it so readily.

"I had no idea you were so interested in me."

"I'm not. I'm interested in the Silvers." She leaned forward. "The Silvers never do anything without a reason. Either they told you or they didn't. If they didn't tell you, then they're playing you. If they did tell you and you're not telling me, then you're playing me." Her frown deepened. "I don't like being played, Mandarin."

I didn't answer. I took a donut and bit into it. I had been right not to trust it. Stale. I put the uneaten part back on the plate.

Mom frowned at me. "We already know there's something going on. Three Silvers went up the hill yesterday. That's unusual enough for even a blind man to notice. So you're not telling me anything I don't already know." Her frown deepened even more, something I hadn't thought possible. I assumed that was her thinking face.

"Fukkit," she said. "You're useless. Go home."

Declined the offer of a return ride in the troll van. The subway was safer. And marginally better smelling.

The bag lady opposite made a face at me. "You're an idiot," she snapped.

"Probably," I agreed.

"You're him," she said. She fumbled in one of her pouches, brought forth a phone, tapped at it, then held it out. Video showed a blurry figure who might have been me climbing into a dark limo with a Silver woman.

I shrugged.

"Turned 'em down, you did. You're an idiot."

"You want to live forever?"

"Who wouldn't?"

"As a bag lady?"

"What's the alternative?"

"If you don't know that, I can't help you." Stood up as the train slowed. My stop. The door opened. Just before stepping out, I turned back. "And . . . that's not your best disguise, Jackson. Try something else, next time."

"Fuck you."

I stepped out of the subway. The word "idiot" floated after me.

"Asshole," I said, shaking my head, not caring if he heard me or not.

But . . . she'd been right, the Silver girl. It hadn't taken long. Bait, decoy, whatever—I was the new follow-me. All the way to my apartment in West Holy Shit.

Up the escalator, turn right, half a block, turn right, half a block up lonely street—old flat-topped, faded-yellow, two-story, stucco building, dating all the way back to Before. Ugly then, uglier now. People avoid it just on aesthetic grounds. Just the way I want it. Just in time for the afternoon earthquake. Barely enough to rattle the dishes. Barely a three.

Inside and up the squeaking stairs to my flat, I'm the only tenant, the owner too, thinking about a hot shower and a cold beer, maybe even a soak, my stomach still sour from the coffee, shower first, beer second—

Sitting at my front door, the kid. Hunched up, arms wrapped around knees. Scruffy and wrinkled. He looked like an understudy for the Lollypop League. He unfolded himself, leapt to his feet. "You got anything for me, Mandy?"

Shook my head.

"Aww, come on. Word is everywhere. You gotta ride in the dark wagon."

"How old are you, Pappy?"

"Eighty-seven anna day. Happy birthday to me." He held up the baby bottle he carried, half filled with cheap booze, and danced his familiar little jig. That had been his answer for more than two decades, probably a lot longer.

"Then you're old enough to know when there's nothing to know. Beat it." I tossed him a coin.

He snatched it out of the air and started to skip down the steps.

"Wait—" I called after him.

He stopped, looked back.

"Make a deal?"

"Always listening, Mandy . . . ?"

"Exactly. You hear anything about anything, you tell me, okay?"

"Innit for me?"

"Birthday present." Nodded toward the bottle. "Something for the baby."

"Deal." He skipped down the stairs, singing to himself. "Baby, baby, baby. Oh, baby, baby, baby . . ."

Finally inside. Dropped my phone on the table. Face down, so it wouldn't ring.

"Hello, Man . . ." Her voice husky as a chainsaw.

Whirled around. Glowered. "Melody."

She flashed her pearlies. "In the flesh." She had poured herself into my favorite chair, one leg draped over the other like a pause in a seduction.

"So," I said. "You had a dupe made before you returned my key?"

"That's what I've always admired in you, Man. Your grasp of the obvious."

"Yes, thanks. See yourself out, willya?"

She ignored the invitation. Instead, she ran her fingers through her unnaturally yellow hair, shook it in a way that she assumed was seductive. I ignored the invitation.

"The Silvers are still after you."

"I went for a ride. I had a glass of water."

"That's not what I heard."

"Then you heard more than me."

"Really . . . ?"

"Melody, I'll tell you everything I told everyone else. There's nothing to tell. And even if there were, I wouldn't tell you. Now, go away." I pointed toward the door. "I'm tired, my back hurts, and I want a shower."

She stood up, unbuttoning the top button of

her dress. "Want your back scrubbed . . . ?"

"Yes, but not by you." I grabbed her elbow and pushed her toward the door. "I still didn't get the knife out from the last time." Pulled the door open, shoved her out. "Don't come back." Closed the door firmly. Hadn't even finished locking the deadbolt before the knocking began.

"I said, 'Don't come back!'"

"Mandarin." Deep voice, guttural.

"Shit." I began unlocking. Opened the door. "Now, what?" I was staring into someone's chest. A black suit. And a holographic ID card held in a fist the size of my head. There were two of them, but the door was only wide enough for one at a time. The second one was larger, he had to turn sideways to get in. And stoop a little too.

"Yeah. I should have expected."

"We have a standing order to investigate all civilian contact with the Silvers."

"I know."

"You wanna sit? This might take a while."

"I've got nothing to tell you that I didn't already tell Mom. There's nothing."

"No problem," said the first. He nodded to the second.

The second was carrying a black case. I hadn't noticed it before. "This won't hurt," he said, already opening it. Pulled out a hammer-hat.

"Yeah, I've heard that before."

Second pushed me down onto a kitchen chair, pushed the rig firmly down onto my skull and secured the chin strap. "Just relax."

"I know the drill. Lie back. Think of England."

"What's England?"

"Never mind. Before your time."

Second studied the screen inside the lid of the case. "Count back from a hundred, give me a baseline."

"A hundred bottles of beer on the wall, a hundred bottles of beer . . ."

"Don't be funny." A hint of a threat?

Too tired to argue. Red was right, I'd been beaten up and beaten down. Broken. "One hundred . . . ninety-nine . . . ninety-eight . . . ninety-seven . . ."

"That's good," he said.

". . . twenty-three . . . twenty-two . . ."

"You can stop now. We have everything we need."

"That was quick," I said.

"Maybe for you," First said. "Either they blanked you or you're telling the truth. Nothing happened."

Felt my eyes narrowing. Second was removing the rig now. Looked past him at First. "They didn't blank me."

"Not that you'd know."

Lifted my hands in a small gesture of submission, agreement. "Okay, you got nothing. Right?"

"We're not allowed to tell you."

"You pick stuff out of my head and you're not allowed to tell me what you picked? Funny."

"Very. We'll laugh about it all the way home."

Second closed his case and straightened. "You ready?" he said to First.

"Yeah."

I locked the door behind them, leaned my head against it for a long moment. Didn't know whether to laugh or sigh. But at least nothing could keep me from my shower now.

Nothing except a dead body in the tub.

THREE

The body was headless.

A skinny boy. Naked. Milk-white skin. By the look of the pubes, a redheaded boy. Late teens, probably. It took me a moment to make even that identification, because of all the blood.

"Oh, fuck. Fuck, fuck, fuck, fuck, fuck." I stepped back carefully, went back to the table, grabbed my phone and called Mom. "Things just got a lot more interesting over here. There's a dead body in my tub."

"Whose?"

"As long as it's not mine, I don't care."

"Wrong answer. Try again."

"Headless redhead."

"Have you looked in the fridge?"

"No. I'm not going near it."

"I'm sending a team. Don't touch anything." She clicked off and I sank down in my chair. It still smelled of Melody's perfume, but I was too tired to move.

Almost ten years ago, there had been seven redhead murders. All young men between the ages of 17 and 27. Slight enough not to be a physical challenge in a fight. Never more than a month apart.

Their headless bodies were each found in a bathtub, savagely stabbed, multiple times. The bodies were never found in their own home or apartment, they were all found in the home or apartment of someone connected to law enforcement or reporting on law enforcement. A high-ranking detective who'd led the investigation of a celebrity homicide, a particularly nasty legal commentator, a beat officer who'd accidentally caught a killer while writing a ticket for an expired registration, a filmmaker who specialized in murder documentaries, a psychiatrist who studied serial killers, and a couple others. The profilers said the redhead killer was playing a particularly sophisticated game of "catch me if you can."

The news of the murders went viral after the third victim. When redheaded men started dying their hair blond, brown, black, or even shaved their heads, the murders stopped.

I grabbed a notebook and a pen from the table. I'm old-fashioned. I think on paper. I started writing questions.

Same killer or copycat?
Why me? Why now?
Related to Silvers? If so, how?

Who's the boy?

How did murderer and boy get in without being seen?

<u>Why</u> the murder? Why <u>here?</u>

What's in the fridge?

Where is Katt?

There were other questions, but I wasn't going to write them down. These were enough to consider right now.

First—and most important. "Katt? Come on out."

No answer.

Pulled out phone. "Locate Katt."

The screen showed a radar display with an arrow pointing in the direction of the couch. "Last known location of Katt."

Got up, crossed, looked behind couch. Dead Katt. Unrecognizable. A scattering of wires and plastic intestines. And a smell of scorch.

Not surprised, just annoyed. Katt had been expensive, top of the line. My phone showed that its feed to the offline storage ended in an abrupt scramble shortly after the troll had dragged me off to see Mom. The Katt had probably been EMP-ed through the door and then personally smashed by someone or something's anger. I doubted that a forensic reconstruction would reveal anything useful. Katt's killer was an expert. He'd probably used a tight beam to avoid taking out anything else—which would have created the kind of anomaly that would have attracted unwanted attention.

That big a localized failure, the monitors would have howled for the cops.

Damn. I'd almost been fond of that Katt. I'd had it long enough for it to start growing a personality. Insurance would cover replacement, of course, but next time I'd need to invest in a better unit, maybe even a Raptor, those are armored. And they're licensed to attack.

Could I afford it? Out of curiosity, I checked my bank balance. How much had the Silvers paid me for my time?

Blinked. Really? *That* much?

So they were serious. I could buy a whole ecology of bots now. I sat back down in my chair. This was a lot bigger than I realized.

I needed time to think. When Mom and her team got here, there'd be a lot of questions. They'd tape off the whole building. I could get a motel room, but it might be better to head for the safe house. Not probably—certainly. Make myself hard to find for a while. Way too much attention since—

I picked up the notepad and looked at my list.

Lists are good. Lists are useful.

Turned to a blank page and started scribbling. Two columns this time.

Me	Everyone else
Meeting with Red	
	?? watching?
Sleep in car	?? arrives, kills
Troll drags me	

out
(20 min ride?)
Meeting with
Mom
(30 min?)

Katt
?? enters flat
?? kills boy
(20 min?)
(30 max?)
?? leaves

Melody arrives,
waits
Jackson on
subway

I finish with
Mom
Take subway
home
(15 min?)

Pappy at door

I get home
Melody (10
min)
Feds (30 min?)
Feds leave
Find body in
tub

All those people should have been tripping over each other. The whole thing looked as meticulously choreographed as the thousand robot dance number at the Super Bowl halftime.

And it all started with the meeting with Red —probably set in motion within minutes of my getting in the dark limo.

Went back to the first page and drew a line through the second item.

~~Why me? Why now?~~

Why me? Because I got into the goddamn car.

Why now? Because I got into the goddamn car.

Went back to the second page and studied the timeline.

The chatter must have been immediate.

Pappyjack was an opportunist. He'd heard noise, he came sniffing for crumbs. I could set him aside for the moment. Melody, likewise. She wanted more than crumbs though, she wanted the whole cookie.

Next page.

Killer doesn't arrive until I leave. Tracking me? Yes.

Feds show up after I get home. Also tracking.

Jackson on subway? Too convenient. Probably working off tip.

Who else is tracking?

Mom. Yes.

Silvers? Probably. But how?

At least three, possibly five monitoring me.

More???

Who else?

Everyone who follows the chatter.

Next page.

Put pen to paper, but didn't write.

Crap.

Put pen down. This was stuff I couldn't write down. Because I couldn't depend on keeping my notes secure.

The boy had been killed less than two hours ago. That meant that whoever killed him had to have had time to plan. How much time do you need to arrange a murder?

How much time to set up a copycat murder?

First, find one redhead.

Figure the killers would not have decided a murder was necessary until after I poured myself into my car. An hour? Two?

Then, how long to find the redhead boy? Another two or three hours? Probably one of the clubs on Santa Monica. By then it would have been dawn. A restaurant? A gym?

Too difficult to find the right redhead on such short notice. Had to have had a couple on the shelf, to be ready for just this kind of situation. And the necessary *equipment* in a bag, ready to go. Gloves, apron, mask, knives . . .

So when did the killer get the redhead boy? Did he already have the redhead trussed up in the back? Or maybe he was a delivery boy? Deliver yourself here, big tip if you're on time. That would have to wait until the coroner identified the body.

Went back to the timeline.

If the killer brought redhead with, then earliest time he could have entered flat would have been when I was pushed into Mom's office. If redhead sent to this location, then killer would have been watching, waiting for me to leave.

Hm.

Killer had to have known Mom was going

to have me picked up. Did he have a mole in the department? Nah. Didn't need it. If the murderer was smart enough to know the location of my flat, smart enough to EMP my Katt, smart enough to unlock my door, then he was probably smart enough to know that Mom would have me picked up after a meeting with the Silvers.

Hell, anyone who gets a ride up the hill and comes back down afterward gets a free ride to see Mom. No mystery there.

Okay.

Why were the feds so late in showing up? Were they giving the killer(s?) time to finish? No. Don't assume a connection—then you have to assume a conspiracy. That way is madness.

Feds versus Mom? Jurisdictional issue? Or maybe they had to go to their office and have a meeting first. Get briefed. And they'd need a warrant for the data dump. And some backstory on me as well, for a baseline. Figure an hour at least to prep. Fifteen minutes enroute? Okay, the timing worked.

Footsteps were thundering up the stairs. Mom's team. I closed the notebook and put it in my coat pocket. My pen as well.

There was another thought I needed to pursue, but it would have to wait. Not *who* had killed a Silver, but *how.*

FOUR

Momma's boys are thorough. Give them credit for that.

They showed up dressed for haz-mat. Puffy white ghosts, like a team of marshmallow men. Accompanied by a herd of sniffer-bots and a flock of skyballs to umbrella the building. They didn't miss a trick. I sat and watched until they told me to stand. They scanned and sniffed me, then the chair, then me again. Then they told me to sit down again. "Stay there, please."

They disappeared into the bedroom, then the bathroom. They were in there a long time. They checked the closets. They looked under the furniture. They scanned and sniffed the dead Katt behind the couch. They scanned the fridge, but didn't open it.

When they were finally through, Mom arrived.

"Pardon me for not standing. They told me not to move."

She frowned. "You can get up now."

Okay. I stood.

Mom sniffed the air, her frown deepened. "*She* was here?"

Nodded. "And Pappyjack. And the feds. Also Jackson on the subway. All I needed was a Grand Marshall, I could have had a parade."

"All right. Walk me through it."

We went into the part of the flat that functioned as a dining room. Mom sat me down with my back to the refrigerator. She pulled out a recorder. "Talk."

I told her everything—Jackson, Pappyjack, Melody, the feds. Plus my thinking about the timeline as well. We went through it three times. Four. I knew the drill. Part of it was to see if my story remained consistent. Part of it was because each time through, I might remember something else. And part of it was just to annoy the hell out of me. But I had a great alibi. I'd been with Mom the whole time the murder was being committed.

Finally, Mom frowned and slapped the recorder off. She called to her team. "All right, I'm done with the witness. Let's open the fridge." She frowned at me. "You want to stay for this?"

"What I want has nothing to do with it. Open it." I swiveled around in my chair.

Two guys in hazmat suits gave the fridge one more scan-and-sniff. Then Mom reached out and pulled the door open.

A half empty jar of mayonnaise. A squeeze

bottle of mustard. Some ancient bologna. Half a loaf of stale rye bread. The usual.

And a large glass bowl. A bloody head. Red hair. Eyes open, staring in silent amazement. Sudden death does that.

And nine bottles of beer.

"The beer is mine," I said. "But help yourself."

"Not on duty," said Mom.

One of the hazmats began snapping photos with a holographic camera. We waited until he finished and stepped out of the way.

"Do you recognize him?"

Shook my head.

We both stood there a long moment, studying the cold tableau. I didn't know what Mom was thinking. I was just glad I'd headed for the shower first instead of the beer. Seeing this—

—no. The body in the tub was just as bad.

Maybe that was the point.

"It's about disturbing your comfort," I said.

"Huh?"

"It's about drop-kicking you head-first out of your comfort zone. I came home thinking about a hot shower and a cold beer. Whichever one I chose, I was going to get an ugly surprise. Now that I've seen both, I can't decide which is worse. I can clean the fridge, but it'll be a long time before I can reach for a beer without having this picture in my head. Same for the shower. I can scrub the tub —but every time I go into that bathroom, I'll see that body again. I'll think about that murder every time I grab a beer or take a shower or a bath. *That's* the intention. The placement of the body parts has been deliberately calculated to inflict a violent emotional shock—not just the immediate shock, but one that imprints and lasts forever."

Mom frowned, nodded. "Two profilers said the same thing."

"It's one thing to say it. It's another to see it."

"You might want to find another place to live."

"Already on that." Definitely the safe house. Have to abandon the car as well. And probably most of my clothes. Easier than debugging.

"You want a beer?" Mom asked. She waved toward the fridge.

"Huh?"

"It's going to be a while before you can take a shower. We'll be processing the scene all day."

"I'm not going to stay."

"We'll call you if we need you."

But I didn't get up. That *other* thought was coming back to me now. The one I wasn't going to share with Mom.

Why me? Why now? Because of the Silvers. Because I'd gotten into that goddamn car. The red-headed boy's murder was part of it. It wasn't a random bit of bad luck—well, maybe for him, but not for me. No. All of this was connected. The killer wanted to make a point. A very strong and very deliberate and very unmistakable point.

I leaned back in my chair, steepled my hands in front of my face, thinking.

Frowning, Mom slapped a bottle of beer down on the table in front of me. She sat down opposite and waited.

I ignored her. But not the beer. Beer is beer.

The Silvers had invited me up the hill to send a message. Not just send it—broadcast it to the city.

The murder was the reply. Broadcast to the whole world. Here's my answer. Fuck you.

And I'm the channel. Great. I put the beer down.

My expression must have changed. "What?" Mom said.

Shook my head. "Not yet."

"It's about the Silvers, isn't it?" she said.

"Stop reading my mind."

"I stopped reading your mind a long time ago. It made my brain hurt." She frowned. "There's a connection between them and this. Isn't there?"

"Might be." I shrugged. "The timing is . . . reason enough to be suspicious."

Mom frowned. That was her only expression. "You always shrug when you're hiding something. What are you not saying?"

Another shrug. "I'm not saying what I'm not saying."

Mom's frown deepened, more than before. She had a whole repertoire of frowns, each one with a different meaning. Most of them meant she

DAVID GERROLD

was pissed at me.

The coroner's men showed up then. Yellow hazmat suits. Mom frowned at them too. "Everything's processed. Go ahead. Take the body."

Mom had trained her boys well. Nobody talked when she was in the room unless it was absolutely necessary. There were no wisecracks, no jokes, no comments at all. One of them bent to the fridge and gently lifted out the glass bowl containing the boy's astonished head.

Mom was still watching me. She saw the change in my expression. "What was that?"

"That's not my bowl."

She turned and looked, then frowned back to me.

"Are you sure?" To the team, "Guys, wait a minute. Bring that over here."

I'm not squeamish, I've eaten my own cooking, but this wasn't anything I wanted to get close to. The bowl was big, a foot in diameter, maybe more. It was translucent glass, a pale shade of blue, and it was streaked with blood. "I know what's in my kitchen," I said. "I've never seen that bowl before." I explained, "It looks expensive. And it's tasteful. When have I ever spent a nickel I didn't have to? And when have I ever had that kind of taste?"

Mom considered the bowl for a long moment. She waved the team off, waited until they'd left, then turned back to me. "The killer brought his own bowl?"

"No, he had the victim bring it. 'Hey, dead boy. Pick up a bowl big enough to hold your head.' Yes, the killer brought it. It's too deliberate. It has to be part of his . . . statement, presentation, profile, whatever. I think it means something."

"You sound pretty sure."

"Just something about the bowl." A thought occurred to me. "Someone walking down the street with a beautiful glass bowl, maybe someone noticed? I would have."

"I'll have the uniforms ask around the neighborhood."

"What about the other murders? Same kind of bowl?"

"I'll have to check. What are you thinking?"

"If it's the same killer, then he has his own way of doing things. If this bowl doesn't match the others, then this isn't the same killer. It's a copycat. Did he use a bowl from the kitchen or did he bring his own?"

"Hm," she said. "Nice catch."

"Let's just say I have a personal interest in this case now. I don't like having dead bodies dropped in my bathtub. Or heads in my fridge." I picked up my beer. It was too warm to finish. I put it back down.

"I'll see if we can track the bowl," Mom said. "It's upscale enough. It might have a history."

"It'll be a dead end," I predicted. "This killer knows what he's doing."

"Probably. But we'll check it just the same."

She glanced around the room. "All right. I have everything I need from you. Go find someplace to shower and sleep. Don't leave town."

"How long till the tape comes down?"

"A week. A month. I'll let you know." She added, "Go out the back way, the reporters are already gathering out front."

"Yeah, I heard the vans pull up. Thanks."

"And Mandarin—?"

"Yeah?"

"You might want to be a little more careful who you hang out with. What cars you get into."

"Already decided that."

"And wherever you go next—invest in some heavy-duty security. You can afford it now."

Nodded. "Yeah. Thanks to the Silvers, I can afford it. And also thanks to the Silvers, I'm a high-pri target now."

"Just be careful."

"I will. I'm glad you care."

"I don't. I just hate paperwork."

Turned back to her. "Mom."

She looked up.

"This is going to get worse. Much worse."

"Yeah, I know. Everything the Silvers touch —it gets worse."

FIVE

Down the back stairs. Look both ways, cross the alley, duck between the two buildings opposite. Around the corner and into the No-Tel Motel.

Jackie cracked her gum when she saw me come in. "Heard you had a night."

"You haven't heard the half of it."

I slapped a K-note on the counter. "That's for the room in the back." Put another K-note on top of that. "That's for not telling anyone I'm here." Put a third on top of that. "And that's a promise in case someone tries to outbid, I'll double whatever they offer."

She tossed me a key. "Anything else?"

"Call Bobo. I need a rubdown."

Jackie gave me a quick look, then nodded. "Anything else?"

"Ask Bobo to bring a pizza. With everything."

"Should be forty minutes."

"I'll be in the shower."

The room in the back is under the freeway. There's a constant roar of white noise from trucks and traffic. It sounds a little like surf, but not really. I sat down at the desk. Took a moment to calm myself. Took out my phone and laid it face down. Pried off the back, took out the battery, laid it aside.

Took off my shoes, opened the heel of the right and pulled out a new SIM card. From the heel of the left, a new battery. This wasn't going to stop a determined hacker tracing calls through the local cell tower, but by the time he figured out what I had done, that knowledge would be useless.

Popped in the new card and battery. Turned on the phone, dialed one number. Waited for a connect, then immediately clicked off. Pulled out the SIM card and battery, snapped the card in two and put all the pieces in my jacket pocket. Put the old SIM card and battery back in the phone and dropped the phone in the trash can.

Somewhere, a coded signal was flashing back and forth across worldwide web, bouncing from hither to yon, there and back again, surfing the bitwaves. Looking like any other email, a row of electronic dominoes was quietly toppling, each email triggering ten more, a hundred more, until thousands, millions, tens of millions were rippling back and forth across the planet—eventually only a few of the umpteenth generation of signals would arrive at the destination, where they would be collated and analyzed for authenticity. Satisfied, it would trigger a whole other set of actions. I glanced at my watch as I removed it. Three minutes, max. The process was unstoppable. Within minutes, money would start moving through an equally untraceable series of one-time-only connections. Dormant accounts would unobtrusively reactivate. Carefully prepared identities would silently awaken.

It wasn't a perfect escape, but it would buy me time.

I began stripping off my clothes, dropping everything into a dirty pile on the floor. Everything. I kept nothing. Not my wallet, not the money in it, not any of the cards or papers. I took the notebook from my coat pocket, paged through it quickly. Nothing here that needed destroying. Added it to the pile anyway. Shoes. Socks. Pants. Everything. Shirt. Even the bulletproof wrap I wear around my torso. Ten minutes and counting.

Jackie's trust was negotiable. I couldn't depend on it. I had an hour, maybe a little more. She owed me a few favors but I couldn't count on her to stay bought.

Worse, there were two bodies—well, two that I knew of—to demonstrate that there were some very nasty people involved. Confronted with that, Jackie would give me up in a Manhattan minute. In fact, I was depending on her to do just that. Just not right away.

Turned on the TV, loud, and headed for the

hot water. Seven minutes in the room and I was in the shower, leaning against the wall, forehead pressed against the cool tiles, eyes closed and blissing out while hot pulsing jets pounded my back. One thing Jackie hadn't skimped on—a luxury shower. The bed would be equally comfortable, though I hadn't had an opportunity to share it in a while.

Finally, time to think.

Red was a smidge over three-hundred years old. That would have made him one of the late millennials. Not quite the first generation of Silvers, maybe not even second generation, but certainly old enough to be a senior. The red hair and the stocky build suggested a Viking heritage, but not necessarily. Hard to say, not my area of expertise. Whoever he was, he was playing chess on the big board.

Last night he moved a piece. He picked me up there and put me down here.

They said I was bait.

And so far . . .

I should have realized there was another level to it. With the Silvers, there always is. I was a pawn moved forward as a sacrifice.

This morning, the other side moved. Putting a dead body in my bathtub—that was their way of taking the pawn out of play. "No thanks. Not taking the bait." More than that. "This piece is now irrelevant to the game."

Except this piece was pissed as hell. The

murder of the boy—that was *wrong*.

I hate being used. Almost as much as I hate being underestimated. It's the disrespect. I hate being disrespected. Yes, that's my weakness. I'm aware of it.

I was getting used to the heat of the shower, I nudged the temperature up a notch. Not quite scalding, but hot enough to edge into uncomfortable. Closed my eyes again.

Still following the thought—the move had been too obvious from the start. Almost desperate. So it wasn't about bait at all—it was about using me as a decoy to temporarily distract from some other move somewhere else.

That thought left me pissed at the Silvers. More pissed than ever. Because there was a dead boy in my apartment.

I couldn't stop thinking about him. He had a family somewhere, wondering where he was, wondering why he hadn't come home yet. A mom, a dad. Maybe brothers or sisters. Maybe a boy-friend or a girl somewhere? At least, I had been a willing pawn. I got into the dark limo because I chose to. The boy didn't have a choice. He died because someone wanted to take me out of the game. Well, whoever that someone was—bad move. I was in the game for sure now. And making my own moves.

The shower door slid open behind me. Someone very large and very naked stepped in. "Someone ordered a pizza with everything?"

"Sure did."

Bobo's huge hands began kneading my shoulders. "You're tight," he said. He kneaded harder, beyond painful.

"How bad is it?" he asked.

"About as bad as it can be."

"Mm," he grunted. "Full rubdown?"

"Yeah. I think so."

"You want a happy ending?" He slid a hand suggestively around my waist.

"I don't think there's time."

"Damn. You owe me one, sweetheart." He kissed the back of my neck.

"I'm going to owe you a lot more before this is over. I think that's enough for the neck." He reached past me and turned off the shower.

"Stand still." I heard him pick something up from the floor. Something hissed and a stinging cold spray hit my back. A strong smell of peppermint and astringent filled the shower. He sprayed my back, my ass, my legs. But this was only the first coat.

"Turn around," he said.

I did and he began spraying my chest. I recognized the canister, Industrial DeBug, but not the flavor.

"This a new mix?"

He nodded. "Something I've been testing for deep cleaning. I figured you needed more than the usual shpritz. These aren't casual nanos, are they?"

"I don't know what they are. I don't even

know *if* they are. I just can't take any chances."

"How badly were you exposed?"

"They got into the flat. They were there for at least half an hour, maybe more. They killed my Katt."

"Sorry to hear that."

"They had a lot to do."

"They left a mess?"

"Don't ask."

"Don't tell me anything I don't need to know. Close your eyes. Close your mouth. Hold your breath." He began spraying my head. He's a thorough worker. He finished with my hair. "Turn around slowly. Lift your arms." He sprayed up and down my sides. Needles of mint-flavored pain in my armpits.

Bobo's an ex-marine, combat-trained, cast in steel, stamped and molded, a precision instrument with a deceptively easy smile. There are things he doesn't talk about. All I know, he turned down a federal commission and went into business for himself. Personal security consultant—and occasional muscle for hire. Physically augmented, he can walk through a door without bothering to open it first. I assumed he was maxed, I never bothered to ask.

Born male, he'd transitioned to female genitals some time before I knew him, probably in the service, part of the whole augmentation thing. Get rid of everything vulnerable. Tuck it inside and have fun the other way. Some people like that, others are curious. Some are old fashioned. I'm an agnostic.

He worked his way down without saying much. "You're going to lose the last of your body hair. I hope you don't have issues."

Shook my head. "Just want to be bug-free."

"This should do it. Triple-intensity. Ninety-nine percent—cubed. Got some jam in the mix too. Put you way below critical broadcast threshold if there's any residual. Hold out your hands, I want to get between your fingers and under your finger-nails too."

He worked his way down to my crotch with clinical attention. My ass too. He knew this "rubdown" was serious business, he skipped the usual flirtatious remarks, didn't even offer a reach around.

I'd asked him once, "Do you ever miss it? I mean—"

"I'm not missing anything. It's all still here. Just shrunk down to the size of a button and tucked up inside, nice and neat. Okay, it's a lot smaller—ohell, it's a clit now, but all the feeling is still there. It's incredibly sensitive, much more sensitive than having it be the last rubber chicken in the shop, hanging around getting scraped and squashed and constantly needing adjustment."

"So you prefer it this way—"

"Haven't changed back, have I?"

Bobo interrupted my flashback then. "Put your foot up on my knee. I've got to do your toes now."

After he finished with my feet, he straightened. "One more, Mandy, top to bottom, and we'll be done. Turn around." This time, he allowed himself a friendly pat on my ass, leaving his hand there just long enough to let me know how friendly he could be.

I turned around to face him. "Bobo, if this shit wasn't so serious, I'd marry you."

"Sure, now you say yes."

"I'd have said yes a long time ago, but you always want to be the girl."

"That's because I'm better at it than you," he said, very matter-of-factly. "But if you don't get killed today, I'm going to take that as a commitment. Now turn around and let me finish."

Finally, he shut off the spray. "Wait two minutes, then rinse." He stepped out of the shower. I closed my eyes and began counting silently. I'd wait three minutes. In the other room, I could hear Bobo methodically spraying. Jackie wouldn't like that. She'd have to reinstall all her own bugs.

Yes, she promised a clean room. By her definition, a clean room was one that nobody *else* had wired. I knew what she was doing. She had a profitable sideline in data mining. I'd never used the clean room at the No-Tel Motel as anything but a changing station, the first of several. But this would be the last time Jackie would see me, at least in this persona. Things had gotten too dangerous.

"Fuck."

I suddenly realized something. I should have seen it sooner.

"Goddammit."

"You okay?" Bobo called from the other room.

"Yeah. I just realized how stupid I am."

"You should have asked me. I could have saved you the trip."

I didn't answer. I stood in my peppermint-astringent funk, watching the entire revelation unfold.

The redheaded boy—that horrible gruesome murder.

And the bowl.

The translucent bowl, pale blue.

Yes, it was a message. But it wasn't just a message about me. There was too much more to it. In fact, I was probably the only human being on the planet who could see the connection.

It was a message for Red.

A stocky red-haired man who sat in a garden paved with pale blue light.

The message: I—*we?*—kill redheads.

Red said he was playing chess on a gigantic playing field. There was someone, or a whole lot of someones, sitting on the opposite side of the board.

Red said he was playing on a team of five. Whoever he was playing against—I could call them the blacks, or were they the whites? This was chess, wasn't it?—they were a team as well. They had to be.

And the redhead murders. All of them. They were part of the game too. They were moves. They were calculated to intimidate Red and his team. All the previous murders? A different part of the game. Something had happened ten years ago—and those murders had to have been the same kind of intimidation.

They'd only stopped when—what? If the purpose was intimidation, then the Silvers had finally taken the threat seriously and backed off. So there was no need for any more murders. So why start again now? Either the Silvers were making another play for the same goal—or another one, more threatening to the whites.

Oh, crap.

Think this out. Who could play such a long game against the Silvers? Only another group of immortals. Another group of Silvers? Or were the whites something else? Something unknown.

Crap and double crap.

And if I were the only human being on the planet who could see this connection, then . . . either the whites intended for me to figure it out—or they intended for me to be irrelevant. As in *dead*.

Red had to be aware of that possibility—and he didn't care.

This was crap on a stick and dipped in chocolate.

There was more. The Silver who was killed

had to be part of Red's team. It was the only possible explanation for this whole series of events. Any other Silver—would Red have made this play?

And why such a weird and desperate move? Putting me on the board? No, I was the decoy, a distraction. And anything I did now—even disappearing as I was planning—was part of that distraction.

I realized I was cold. How long had I been standing in the shower? My skin felt gummy. I turned on the water and rinsed off the last of the DeBug. Waited till the air dryers finished blasting. Called to Bobo, "Is it safe to come out yet?"

"All clear."

I grabbed one of the towels Bobo had brought and began drying my hair.

"You okay?" he asked. He'd bagged all of my clothes and put the bag by the door. As soon as we finished here, they'd be ash in some incinerator.

"No. I'm an idiot. I made a stupid assumption." I tossed the towel toward the bag and began finger-combing my hair.

"Assumptions will have you believing things that aren't there," Bobo agreed. He was now wearing a foil jump suit, with matching gloves and hood. He opened the bag and dropped the towel in. He nodded toward the bed where a large flat box waited. "Large pizza, with everything."

Inside it, sealed in plastic, a complete costume change. Clothes, accessories, everything. Bobo laid a plastic sheet on the bed. I laid out the clothes.

My turn to frown.

"Really, Bobo?" I looked at him. "A dress?"

He allowed himself a grin. "Mandy, you're a beautiful woman. How often do I get to see you looking like one? How often does anyone? Did I get the sizes right? Or have you been doing the hot fudge sundae circuit again?"

SIX

Bobo bundled me into the back of the van and drove around the city for a couple of hours. Evasive maneuvers. A predatory sky-bot might be tracking the van. We pulled into a parking structure and switched vehicles, waited fifteen minutes, then pulled out again. We did that three times. Confidence was high, but never high enough.

He finally dropped me off near a darkened subway entrance. We couldn't be absolutely certain that we hadn't been tracked—there are no absolutes, but Bobo had bought me time, enough to go underground. Literally underground.

Down the subway stairs, into the women's restroom, into the third stall on the left, press the third tile down in the third column, squeeze through the opening, grab the rungs of the ladder, close the panel, exhale, and climb down.

At the bottom, the tunnel was dark. It smelled dank and dusty at the same time. No one had been through here in a long time. There were no fresh tracks in the dirt. Good.

In the distance, I felt the vibration of a subway train as it rolled into the station. Or it could have been another shallow tremor. Two or three a day, part of the city's charm. But this was the train. If someone was tracking me, they'd expect me to be on it, activating skybots over every station on the route. The vibrations receded in the distance and I made my way through the passage.

This was a maintenance tunnel, wide enough and tall enough for two trucks to pass. One wall was for electrical and communication cables, the other for water and sewage conduits. Water above, sewage below.

Still counting, I stopped at the fourteenth panel on the right. The door next to it slid open, revealing an equipment locker. Stepped in quickly, slid the door shut, and spoke the passcode aloud. The left side of the locker swung open, revealing a short parallel corridor, lined with lockers. At the end of it, a narrow closet.

The Silvers weren't the only ones with secrets, although I suspected that they knew more of our secrets than we knew of theirs—because we knew none of theirs. At least, I didn't. If anyone else did, they hadn't told me.

I pushed the closet open.

Sanctuary was a hole left over from the construction of something or other, a forgotten temporary office, now reopened, reinforced and triple-shielded, with no direct communications in or out. Jamming walls prevented any and all bugs from sending or receiving signals. Heat-barriers protected against thermal imaging. Sonic insulation prevented vibration sensors from measuring or weighing the contents. Microwaves and X-rays were also blocked. At the moment, it housed a community of one. Me.

The lights flickered on above me. The chamber was spare and utilitarian. But it was warm and it was secure. I stripped quickly, dropped my clothes into the disposal. My new accessories were still sealed in plastic. Unless Bobo had been compromised, they were clean, but I tossed the bag into the basket anyway. The bag would be sprayed, then scanned.

I punched for detox and stood under the spray. It was unlikely that I'd been hacked somewhere enroute, but I couldn't take the chance. Not even an ad-bug. This time it didn't tingle—it *stung.* I held up my arms and turned slowly.

Finally, the air jets blasted me dry. A drawer popped open, offering a pale blue—*did it have to be that color?*—robe. I removed it from the plastic and slipped into it easily. At least it was soft and comfortable. Grabbed my accessory bag and put my hand up to the wall panel. The door to the sanctuary slid open. I stepped across the threshold with an audible sigh of relief—

She was sitting on the couch. Silver hair, porcelain skin. Cold gray eyes, the color of the evening sky.

Goddammit.

"I paid a lot of money for this sanctuary. It's supposed to be Class-Nine Secure."

"It still is."

"Then it was sold to me under false pretenses. I wanted a safe house secure from the Silvers."

"We'll refund your money. Plus interest."

"That's very comforting."

"That's sarcasm, right?"

"Nice of you to notice."

"Mandarin," she said quietly. "The situation has changed."

"A dead boy in my bathtub, his head in my fridge, in a pale blue bowl. Yeah, I'd say the situation has changed. Somebody wants me derailed. That same somebody wants to send a message to Red. And whoever that somebody is—it's probably a lot of somebodies. And they probably have enough power to be a genuine threat to the Silvers."

Her face remained expressionless.

"Yes, I figured it out. How could I not? It's what I do. Red. Red-haired boys. Pale blue bowl. Pale blue paving stones. Unsolved serial killings with bodies showing up in the bathtub of anyone in contact with the Silvers? Someone's building a deadly firewall. They want to put a fence around you, keep you from doing whatever it is you're trying to do in the human world. Even a one-eyed TV detective could see it. Why aren't they eliminating the people directly? Because that'd be too obvious. You don't want the feds looking into this."

"Have you told Mom any of this?"

"Mom knows I talked to Red. That much. I don't think she knows the importance of the bowl. But she certainly knows that there are Silver strings attached."

"Mandy—"

"Don't call me that."

"This is not what we intended—"

"Well, gosh."

"They broke the truce. There weren't supposed to be any more killings."

"Who are *they?*"

She stopped. "I can't tell you that."

"Can't? Or won't?"

"Both."

We sat in silence for a bit, both staring at each other. She was beautiful—and beyond reach. I was—well, probably disheveled and sorely human. I could see that she was studying me, but whatever was going on behind those cool gray eyes—it was unfathomable. The silence annoyed me, but I had nothing to say. And she wasn't going to give me any information that she didn't want me to have.

Finally, "Why are you here?"

"You're in danger."

"I kind of figured that."

"No. Not the kind of danger you're thinking."

"I'm the only human being on the planet who knows the Silvers are at war with . . . somebody or something. Whoever they are, they have to know I've figured it out. Just by going underground, I've given myself away. So if you don't want me dead, they do."

"They don't want you dead."

"No?"

"No." She said it quietly. "They want to assimilate you. And unlike us, they won't give you a choice. You'll go to sleep one night, you'll wake up the next morning, you'll be one of *them*."

"How do you know I'm not already?"

"If you were, I'd have killed you when you came in."

"Well, thank you for not killing me."

"I didn't want to come. But I didn't want anyone else doing it either."

"Like putting down a beloved pet?"

"Mandy—"

"You should go."

"We're not done."

"We were done a long time ago."

"I understand," she said. "I understand better than you realize. I know it hurt. I know it still hurts. I know it hurts to see me like this."

"We've had this conversation before. Why do we have to have it again? You chose *them* instead of me. How could that *not* hurt?"

"And why are you still carrying the hurt around? When will you let go of it?"

"When I die." That should have stung her, but it didn't. "What do you want from me?"

"I want you to know what's available on *this* side."

"That's not going to happen. As far as I'm concerned, the Silvers are thieves. The choice they offered you, they had to know what they were doing to us."

"They expected you to come along."

"Well. *Quelle* surprise. The Silvers aren't perfect. They made an assumption."

"So did I," she said. "I thought you would come with me."

"No," I said. "I want you to understand something." I took a breath. "Despite everything you might want me to believe, you're still human. Augmented in ways I can't imagine. Transformed. But still human. With all the faults and weaknesses and kinks of humanity—only this time raised to the level of dispassionate arrogance. If a cockroach climbs a ladder, it might have a higher perspective, but it's still a cockroach. Did it ever occur to any of you that maybe, just maybe, there are some of us who don't want to go on your ride? We want to go on our own." I looked across at her. "And don't tell me you understand—because you don't. You gave up *this* understanding when you crossed over."

"Are you done?"

"No." I thought about it. "Yes."

"All right. Now it's my turn." She took a

breath. "Do you know how painful it is for me to talk to you?"

That stopped me. I closed my mouth.

"When I talk to you, I have to stop being the all of me that is. I have to be the part of me that *was*." She hesitated, considering her next words. "This is why Silvers do not spend much time with humans. We have to become less than ourselves. It's not—it's not pleasant. It's cramped. So we only do it where there's a compelling reason."

"How superior of you."

"It's not arrogance, Mandy. It's something else—the closest human word is *pity*."

"Pity sounds pretty arrogant to me."

"Then try sorrow. We know how difficult the ladder is. Not everyone climbs it."

"That sounds arrogant too."

She looked across at me, suddenly hard. "Mandy! Shut the fuck up!"

Startled, I shut. I'd never heard any Silver speak so directly. And I'd never expected *her* to speak that way to me.

"You need to understand something. The only reason that I am here at all is because—because you are still important." She hesitated.

"You can't say it, can you?"

"I can say it. It wouldn't be accurate. You made it possible for me to be *this*. That makes you important—important to me. You're in danger, Mandy, the worst kind of danger. Worse than death. You deserve more than a warning. You de-

73

serve protection. Come back to the keep."

She stopped. She waited.

I let her wait. I had to gather myself. When I was ready, I let it out. "Every time you do this, every time you reach out to me, it *hurts*. Every time I see you, it *hurts.* Every time you speak to me, it *hurts*. Do you know how much this is hurting me right now?"

"Yes, I do."

"And you still can't say it?"

"I'm sorry? No, I can't say it. Because I'm not sorry. I can't apologize for what I chose. I won't apologize for doing what's necessary. I learned that from you. Remember?"

"I remember," I said. "I remember everything. Maybe not as well as you can, but I remember enough."

"Come back to the keep with me."

"I don't think so."

"You'll be safer there."

"Safer? Not safe? Just *safer?*"

She ignored the question. "There are things you need to know."

"I already know too goddamn much. That's why I'm in danger. If I'm that fucking important to you, why did you and Red put me in this position?"

"Because it was necessary."

I stood up. I don't know if I think better when I'm pacing, but I know I speak more honestly. "Do you know why I can't let go of you? As much as I want to, as much as I've tried, I can't—

because you won't let go of me. You keep coming back to me. Again and again. You're the one who won't let go."

"We're having two different conversations," she said.

"Yes, I know. You're having the conversation you want to have and I'm having the one I need to have. We were always having two different conversations. That's why you left me."

"Yes, that's how it looked to you."

"That's what you said the day you left."

"Because that was how it looked to me. At the time." She stood up. "It's time to go. Are you coming?" She held out a hand.

I looked at her outstretched hand. Looked to her face. Looked inside myself. Looked back to her. Went to the wrong question. "How much danger am I in?"

"Your sanctuary here—" She gestured, indicating the room. "It has been compromised." She let that sink in.

"How do you know that?"

"I'm here, aren't I?"

I couldn't argue with that.

Fuck.

SEVEN

The queasy sensation in my stomach suddenly crystallized. Another piece was about to fall into place.

"You led them here," I said.

"What?"

"You weren't careful enough!"

She looked puzzled. A strange expression on her face.

"How do you know that—?"

"The alarm is about to go off—"

The end of my sentence was cut off by an ear-piercing screech. All the lights went red. One wall cleared and became a giant schematic display with a red dot moving through one of the corridors.

"Everybody tracks the Silvers. *Everywhere!*" I dropped my robe and ran to the closet. Yanked out a jumpsuit. Tossed a second one to her. "We've got maybe two minutes." Started pulling it on. "Silvers don't care if they get tracked. Nobody knows what you're up to anyway. You're deliberately obscure everywhere. And nobody kills a Silver—they can't, they won't, they're afraid to. But everybody you talk to is always at risk. You people are a moving plague zone."

Give her credit. She didn't argue. She zipped up the jumpsuit and flipped the hood over her head, finishing the same time I did. Augmented co-ordination shows up as speed. Good for her.

The wall display changed to reveal the view down the tunnel. Something dark was moving at the far end. Something large and dark. And heavy. The camera view was shuddering with every foot-step. It thumped, it thundered, it boomed. The impact resonated through the floor, the walls, the ceiling, shaking the projector too.

"It's a tunnel troll—"

"I thought those were—"

"Well, they're not—" The thing was visible now, filling the entire width of the tunnel and it still had to crouch low, moving slowly and pon-derously forward on all fours. It braced itself on its knuckles and hunkered forward, snorting and snuffling as it came. "They're vets. Leftovers from the war. Mostly, they stay deep. Who knows what they've carved out beneath the city?"

"They were supposed to be cleaned out."

"Yeah. Well, you build a war machine—it takes a bigger machine to take it down. And then what do you do with that machine? It's cheaper to say, 'Y'know what? Maybe we should keep a few of these things around, just in case. We'll bury them deep so no one will know.'"

The tunnels had residual lighting, but they were still gloomy. Even with light amplification and image-enhancement, the troll still showed up on the display as a large dark hulk, almost devoid of detail. It moved slowly, but its size was deceptive. It was heading directly toward the camera—directly toward *us*.

I glanced over at her. "So there are things the Silvers *don't* know?"

She nodded.

"That's reassuring."

"We aren't everywhere." She studied me. "You seem awfully calm. You have a plan?"

"I've never tested it."

"Now would be a good time."

"I need to let it get closer."

"How close?"

The troll's sharp features filled the wall now. It roared, revealing rows of jagged broken teeth all the way back. It turned its great flat head from side to side, eyeing the wall before it with baleful curiosity.

It reached out with one great claw and scratched slowly and tentatively at the concrete, testing it deliberately, carving deep gouges with its diamond-hard claws. Another scratch and another and then it was methodically and patiently digging with both gigantic paws. The surface crunched and shattered with every measured scrape. Huge pieces fell. The troll grunted and growled with the effort, a deep guttural booming moan of determination—a slow-motion avalanche of hunger.

The surface of the display shuddered and shook. The image bulged as the wall behind began to crack.

"*That* close," I said. "Cover your eyes."

The wall collapsed downward, large pieces sliding off the troll's back as it lurched into the space formerly known as sanctuary. I put my hands up in front of my face. The projectors blazed behind me—a whole wall of light, howling so bright that even facing away from it I could still see the bones of my hands through my clenched eyelids, even through the light-blocking plastic of the hood. And that was just the ambient reflections—

The troll roared in agony, yelping backward in reaction, struggling to shield its face, turning its head away and waving its gigantic claws, trying desperately to ward off the piercing dazzle. The monster backed away, step by clumsy step, angrily retreating, bellowing and growling with both pain and rage—

—and that's when the harpoons fired, a rapid tattoo, thunking into the troll from three different angles.

The troll thundered, rising up on its squat hind legs, waving its front claws in protest. Despite the pain, it charged—

DAVID GERROLD

The embedded heads of the harpoons detonated in a dozen simultaneous cold-fusion explosions. The troll froze, *literally*, as the superfluids flooding its tissues reduced its cells to ice, shattering them outward in crackling waves of burning cold.

The troll trembled, collapsed, shattered, splashed, and puddled with a choking roar, a grunt, and a gurgle. The whole mess bubbled. The stink was . . . beyond description, a stench of garbage and decay. And a few unnamable things even worse than that.

"You didn't have to kill it," said Silver.

"No, I didn't." I had trouble getting the words out. I was still blinking in the fading glare, still trying to steady my breathing.

"The lights would have been enough to drive it away," she said. Both her voice and her breathing were steady.

"Uh-huh," I agreed. "The lights would have been enough."

"But you killed it anyway."

"See? You don't understand me. Not as much as you think."

"Explain?"

"Too many people have been using me. You. The rest of your . . . whatever. Mom. The feds. The other side, whoever they are. A lot of people have been sending me messages. I just sent one back."

"A dead troll?"

"Mm-hm."

"What message?"

"Stop fucking with me."

"And a dead troll sends that message?'

"Uh-huh. A dead troll is almost impossible to dispose of. And if you think they stink bad when they're alive—well, take a deep breath."

I looked around at the damage. Sanctuary was beyond repair. The outer wall was all caved in. "You'd better make good on that refund," I said. Yanked back the rug, lifted up the hatch in the floor. Pulled out hand-held rocket launchers and ammo belts. Threw half of the gear at her. "Let's go."

"Where—?"

"We have to kill the other one."

"The *other* one—?"

"Yeah. This was only a junior. Senior's gonna be pissed. You don't have a lot of experience with battle trolls, do you?"

"I wasn't in the service—"

"Neither was I. Not officially." I waved an ammo belt at her. "Pick that stuff up. Follow me."

"Mandarin. You're asking me to involve myself in mortal affairs—"

"You don't have a choice. You can't stay here. Containment services are already on their way. You don't want them asking questions, do you?"

She followed me across the rubble of the wall, into the tunnel, still protesting. "You know I can't use these things—" She held up the weapons in her hands.

"I know. You're just the sherpa. Now shut up. I need to listen."

She did and I did.

Far down the tunnel, another troll was thumping and growling. This one was angry. This was momma troll, almost too big to move through the corridor. We had that much in our favor.

"Come on. We have to scramble. Watch out for the tracks. There's no power, but you can still trip over them—"

The spotlight on the weapon was a bright finger of light poking the darkness. Something with red eyes howled at us in the distance, but didn't approach. It just yowled and retreated, only occasionally glancing back. The screen showed me I was locked on the target, but even with a target that large blocking the tunnel confidence wasn't great. I didn't like the range, but I'd have to take the shot anyway.

"We're gonna have to get closer. Come on!"

I didn't wait to see if she was following. I started running toward it. Had to close the distance. Full-grown tunnel trolls are armored like bunkers. One shot wouldn't bring it down, would barely get its attention. But if I could hit a knee, I could immobilize it—and then get close enough to put one in its eye or down its throat.

I had six rockets. She had six. It could be enough. If it wasn't—well, if it wasn't, I'd be in no position to worry about it.

The tunnel curved ahead. The red eyes disappeared. A partial collapse blocked our view around the turn. She touched my arm and whispered, "It's there, crouching low."

"I can't see it."

"I can."

"If I miss, it'll charge us."

"Then don't miss."

"Can't miss. It's blocking the tunnel. But I need to hit it in the right spot."

"How do you know so much about trolls?"

"I just do."

"You fought them—?"

"No." After a bit, I added, "I was a wrangler. No, check that. I wasn't just a wrangler. I was a wrangler who survived."

"How?"

"By quitting. One of the adolescents wanted to mate with me. Okay, I deserted. I told you, there's a lot you don't know about me." I checked the charges on the weapons. "Earned my way back as a consulting expert on eradication after the war."

"Oh."

"Failed that too. The whole program failed. We beat 'em back for a bit, then they went underground. Deeper than anyone wanted to follow. Don't know why these two came up so close to the surface. Something must have awakened them— and really pissed them off. 'Course, that's not hard to do."

There was nothing visible at the far end of

the tunnel. I tapped the panel of the gunsight, expanded the view. It revealed the beam and the bright dot of the targeting laser far beyond the range of visible light. But all I saw was another lump of rubble.

"You've lost it," she said.

Shook my head. "That's it. Camouflage."

Flipped off the safety. Sighted. Squeezed.

The rail-gun whuffed. A brilliant streak sliced the air—a white flash blazed. Colors splattered yellow, orange, red. Flames, dust, clouds, spattering rocks and pebbles. The tunnel shook and howled. Something was impaled.

A second rocket. Sighted, locked, whuffed—and this time, behind the flash the tunnel shuddered and groaned, then crackled, shrieked, and one wall collapsed. The smell of ozone now—the gun was overheating.

The third rocket. We were going to have to retreat, but I needed to get this last shot off—and whuffed. Missed, goddammit. The rocket bounced off the distant wall of the curve and exploded out of sight, flaring white light sideways, illuminating the tunnel troll in a yowling posture of agony and rage—headed toward us now!

"Hand me the other gun. This one needs to cool—"

Fourth rocket. Hard to breathe in all the smoke—and the ozone from the first gun made my eyes water. Never mind that now. Sighted, squeezed—and flashed. Knocked the bastard down

—but not for long. The damn thing scrambled back to its feet and kept on coming.

"Okay, we've got its attention now—"

Another whuffling shot, this one dead center. A perfect flash. The troll slammed backward against the rubble. Another section of wall slid down on it. It waved one arm, futilely pushing at the debris that pinned it.

"You got it—"

"Yeah, I got its attention—"

"It's down—"

"Not for long. I only dazed it."

Sighted on its eyes. Squeezed. Whuffed. Hard to see with all the purple spots in front of my eyes.

"It's up—"

The second gun was overheating now. Grabbed the first one out of her arms. Locked and loaded. Sighted and squeezed. A muted flash. The tunnel was filled with burning dust and choking smoke. Couldn't breathe. She dragged me backward.

"I can't see it!"

"I can. It's down. Not moving." She squinted. "Part of its head is gone. Does that mean—"

"It means we slowed it down—"

"Mandy! A straight answer."

"I don't know!" I shouted back, coughing. New noises rattled in the darkness beyond the smoke. Scrabbling screaming noises. She picked me up, tossed me over one shoulder, a fireman's carry—I didn't know Silvers were that strong. I concentrated on breathing. She concentrated on running.

After a bit, she slowed to a stop. Breathed hard for a moment, then held her breath to listen. "Okay, I know where we are." She lowered me to my feet, pulled the hood off my head, removed her own hood too. "You okay?"

I coughed up phlegm and spat. "I'm going to ask for a refund on these air filters."

"You should."

I blinked tears and dust out of my eyes, straightened. "Got to go back. Finish it off."

"Not necessary. You took its head off."

"Don't you know anything about trolls? The primary brain is in the hindquarters."

"You got it in the ass first. That's why you were able to take off the head."

Something about the way she said it. I looked at her. For a moment, she was almost—no, don't go there. "You sure?"

She nodded. "Leave the guns. Set them for self-destruct. Let's go." She pointed. "That way."

We came out through the women's room of a coffee shop three blocks away. Not my first choice, but good enough. The restaurant was shadowed, night had already darkened the streets. Sunlight replaced by neon glare. I led her to a booth in the back. "Call your car."

"Already done. Are you coming?"

"To the keep? Hell, no!"

"They sent a troll after you—"

"Who the hell are *they?*"

"Not here. It's not secure."

That stopped me. I waved at the blousy waitress. "Two coffees, please." Turned back to *her*. "No place is secure. Not anymore. You proved that."

She didn't answer.

"Here's what I know," I said. "Somebody murdered a Silver. But Silvers can't kill Silvers. Or anything. Not won't. *Can't*. Silvers don't kill. So it wasn't a Silver. But whoever the other side is, they play like Silvers. So they have to be Silvers, but they can't be, so they have to be something like Silvers. Something that can kill—"

She put her hand on top of mine. Firmly. "Don't say any more."

I pulled my hand back. "I don't care who hears. I have a right to be scared. The whole world has a right to be scared. You Silvers should be terrified, you have the most to lose. So I don't care who hears me. Your mysterious *they?* I'm not saying anything they don't already know. The police? Mom isn't stupid. She's got ears everywhere and she can paper the city with warrants. An info-snoop looking for saleable gossip? Hell, there's such a shitstorm of misinformation flurrying around already, you could publish your DNA and nobody would believe it because the bullshit fantasies are so much more exciting."

I pointed at the ceiling. "Every security camera in the city is awake right now. Whatever privacy exists—it exists only for people who are so dull and uninteresting, so mundane that nobody cares. That's not you and it's sure as fuck not me anymore. So thank you very much for that."

She stood up. "My car is here. Last chance."

"What part of 'Hell, no!' didn't you understand the first time?"

"You're not safe down here, Mandy." She headed for the door.

The waitress arrived with the coffees. She blinked after the porcelain woman, confused.

"I'll take 'em both," I said. "And bring me a couple of fresh donuts."

She put them down on the table with a bit of a clatter. "She's one of them—isn't she? What they call Silvers? I never seen one before. Not in person. Wait'll I tell Ducky about this. I waited on a Silver. He'll never believe me. Oh, I shoulda asked for an autograph." She scurried off, twittering like a hypered squirrel.

At least, the coffee was drinkable.

And it gave me a chance to think.

Silvers live long and think fast. Ephemerals live short and think slow. Taking the shine, as they call it, is a good bargain. For anyone else, maybe. Not for me.

And as long as *she* thought it was personal, they wouldn't be asking any other questions.

I pulled out an imaginary notebook and reviewed my imaginary notes. Silvers can't kill, but they can be killed. So whoever killed a Silver wasn't

Silver. It had to be a human. Or a group of humans. But they're playing a long game, like Silvers—and that doesn't make sense. Humans can't play a long game, they don't live long enough.

Ah.

Obvious, really.

Human killers. Silver players. Some kind of alliance. I could almost imagine it. "We'll tell you how to kill Silvers and give you a list of targets. In return—"

In return, what?

That's only one question.

There's also the question of *why*.

And *who*.

I'm not going to find the mysterious *they*. Even the Silvers can't find them. Or they already would have.

And if they had—oh, that was interesting.

If the Silvers knew which Silvers were hiring humans to kill Silvers, then they would hire other humans to kill the Silvers who were hiring humans to kill Silvers.

Well, that complicated things.

And it meant—I had no idea which side I was on. Which side I was being used by.

As if it mattered.

Because this was Silver business, not mine.

And in any case, I'd be very unlikely to find out anything from the Silvers—especially not which Silvers wanted to kill which other Silvers. Let alone why.

Why Silvers did anything was a mystery to everyone—sometimes even Silvers.

So that line of inquiry was pretty much a dead end.

But I might be able to find the humans with dirty hands.

Silvers aren't sloppy, but humans are.

Another question. Silvers fighting Silvers? Really?

Do Silvers have politics?

Do they have politics worth killing over?

If they do, then . . .

Then what? What does that say about their so-called superiority?

Silvers have augmented senses and superior physical abilities. They designed themselves, so they say, for the long ride to the stars.

Until we invent faster-than-light travel, we need the Silvers to take the long ride to other stars. They're immune to the deterioration of muscles, bones, and brain that comes from prolonged exposure to space. And they can sleep for years. When they eventually get to the new world, they'll grow human babies in tanks and raise them to adulthood. Silvers can't reproduce, they need humans to transform.

Three ships were under construction around Luna, three more were planned. But a lot of people had questions. Once they arrived, would the Silvers create a human society? Or would they create their own Silver society with humans as a permanent underclass?

Some people argued we already had that here on Earth—a secret society of Silvers already treating humans as cattle. You couldn't buy your way into the Silver class. Billionaires had tried and failed. If you weren't the right kind of person, if you didn't have the right kind of mind, they said the process of transformation would kill you—if it didn't drive you insane.

I wondered if that was true.

Ahh. Insane Silvers. Maybe that was the *they*. Something the Silvers wouldn't admit, wouldn't discuss.

Obvious, I guess.

Some of the billionaires who'd been turned down had invested hundreds of millions into their own research projects—their own attempt to discover and duplicate the secrets of the immortal uber-humans. But the Silvers had a five-hundred-year head start in genetic engineering. That wasn't going to be replicated in a single human lifetime.

So . . . the alternative was to steal the technology.

Was that possible?

I'd heard that the creation of a Silver required a specific combination of elements. The transformation was a synergistic effect of multiple processes. But that was all anybody knew. And that could be a smokescreen anyway. But if that were the case, then the right mix might be as elusive as the recipe for gramma's stuffed cabbage. You might get close, but you'd never get the same taste.

Assuming you wanted the same taste.

Forget stuffed cabbage.

The billie-boys have resources and they have motivation.

Knowing how to kill a Silver might be a useful clue how to make one. If the billie-boys succeeded in recreating the Silver-transformation, then the Silvers would lose their monopoly. They'd also lose their quality control. And they'd lose their unity as well.

But without quality control, you get insane Silvers . . .

The billie-boys—that's where I should start looking. Except billionaires are even harder to approach than Silvers. And even more dangerous with their power. And besides, the billie-boys wouldn't have committed the murder themselves. They would have hired someone else to do it for them.

Okay, that's two things to look for. Find the murderers or find the secret research facility. No, just one. The facility has to be so well hidden even the Silvers can't find it. It has to be the murderers.

As good as the Silvers are, when a person takes the shine and detaches from humanity, they lose the ability to pass among the folks they left behind. That's their vulnerability. They lose their access to whole domains of human activity, so the Silvers need humans to act for them, humans they can trust.

People like me.

Except I don't want to play that game.

But some people can be bought. That's the place to look. Find out who got bought.

Yeah. Mom needs to know this.

I didn't finish the second coffee. A quick trip to the women's room and I was ready to call for a Yellow Car. Some people still call it the ladies room, but I don't. I'll never be a lady and I don't want to be.

One thing was certain. Secrecy wasn't possible anymore. The only useful action was attack.

If only I knew who.

EIGHT

I went straight to Mom.
Pushed past the troll, strode into the office. She looked up, frowning, and put down the report she was reading.

"Nice jumpsuit," she said. "An improvement. You smell better too."

I sat. "Coffee," I snarled at the troll behind me. "And fresh donuts." It lumbered away, grumbling to itself.

Back to Mom. "Secrecy is impossible. It's an illusion. Everything is an illusion. Illusion is the only reality we have."

Mom nodded. "I see all that money spent on tautology wasn't wasted. What's your point?"

"The redhead killings. They're connected to the Silvers."

Mom hesitated before answering. "We know that. We've known it since the third murder." Her frown faded. "Every single person who found a headless body in their bathtub, they'd had some ongoing contact with one or more of the Silvers, or they had recently been invited to the keep. Two of them had been invited to take the shine. How did you figure it out?"

"Well, the obvious connection was the timing of the body in my tub. The not-so obvious connection is that damn bowl. Pale blue. Translucent. Did you analyze the material?"

Mom frowned. "It's in the lab now."

"It's the same stuff that the keep is paved with."

Her expression froze.

"Yeah," I said. "Think about that for a while."

She steepled her hands in front of her. She closed her eyes. I recognized the position. I'd done it myself, many times. *I need to think about this, what it means.*

The troll arrived with a plastic cup of bitter coffee, even a couple of fresh donuts. I waited until the door slammed behind him.

"Someone has access to Silver tech, some of it anyway," I began. "But it's not a Silver. It can't be. So who has access to Silver technology, but isn't a Silver?"

Mom opened her eyes, frowning again. "You are not the first to ask that question."

"Can we track the bowl?"

"Probably not. These killers don't make mistakes. But we'll make the effort anyway."

"Is it possible that . . ." I let the thought fester a moment. I busied myself with the first donut.

"Could there be a division among the Silvers? Perhaps there are factions? Perhaps the division has become violent? Perhaps one side or the other, or perhaps both, are hiring surrogates to do their dirty work?"

Mom shook her head. "We can't have this conversation here."

"We can't have it anywhere. There's no such thing as secrecy anymore. Somebody sent a tunnel troll after me."

"I heard about that, yes."

"See? That's my point." I spoke with my mouth full, waving the last bit angrily in the air. "Back door exit, triple detox, clean identity, multiple car changes, another detox, and my personal sanctuary was still penetrated by a Silver—*her*—and by the time I get here, you have all the details too. So why are we pretending that anything is still confidential?"

"We can't have that conversation either. Go home." She spoke with finality.

I grabbed my coffee and the second donut. "Okay. You know where to find me." And I was out the door, angry and annoyed. This day was not turning out well. And it was probably going to get worse.

Took the subway west to the beach, came blinking out into the ugly glare of morning. Bright gray sky, gray waves stretching into anonymity. And still the glass sand glittered with rainbow refractions.

Gulls drifted above, skimming for opportunities. A scruffy yellow dog barked at something floating in the water. A ball? Or someone's head. Hard to tell at this distance. Salt-spray smell in the air. And maybe something else as well.

Short walk to the beach house. Too many of the buildings were boarded up, falling into disrepair. After the tsunami, the neighborhood remained mostly deserted, except for squatters, opportunists, and people who still liked the beach. Occasionally a team of demolition trolls showed up to take down one or two of the old structures, but after a while they'd be summoned away for something else and the half-demolished homes remained like a row of broken teeth, grinning ugly.

My building gleamed white. Sometimes I worried that I would return to it, only to find it collapsed in rubble, because some careless troll had misread the address of his team's demolition assignment and proceeded to work, despite the shining green placard high on the front wall.

Trolls. Can't live with 'em, can't shoot 'em. No, really. They're almost impossible to kill.

Unless you have the right ordnance, that is.

Inside, the air was cool and smelled of flowers. I peeled off the jumpsuit and stepped into the bathroom where the hot bath I'd ordered was waiting with a froth of lavender bubbles. I sank into it gratefully. The apartment in the city was convenient, but this was home. And the only body in this tub was mine.

"Yes, I'm bubbling," I said loudly. "And I don't care who knows it. Play some adagios." I sank deeper into the water, submerging completely, only coming up just enough to breathe, letting the heat soak away the tension of the past two days, allowing my mind to drift with the music.

I was annoyed and I knew why I was annoyed. Everything that had happened since *she* showed up—it had happened because of her. Interviewed by Red, dragged in to see Mom, finding a dead boy in my flat, finding her in my safe room, targeted by a tunnel troll, all of it—things that others had done. I'd been treated like a pinball, slammed by the flippers, ricocheted off the bumpers, and hurled back and forth in every direction except the one I wanted to go. I was annoyed because I was being pushed, not doing the pushing.

I wasn't just annoyed. I was pissed off. Ready to push back.

Time to stop. Put it all away.

Go to my happy place instead.

I had one once.

The only problem, *she's* still in it. I can't keep *her* out of anything.

Is she doing that? Or am I?

Am I doing something that keeps dragging her back into my life?

Interesting question, but not answerable. She wanders in and out as she chooses. But why does she keep choosing *me*?

Because I'm the one that got away?

Just like *she* is. Also the one that got away.

Hm.

I gave up. With all this crap swirling around, that particular method of relaxation wasn't going to work. Not this time. And probably not again, not for a long time. She'd ruined that too.

The tub hissed for a bit, cycling, frothing, bubbling some more, and reheating itself back to perfection.

I was still a long way from being relaxed, but no alarms were blaring, nothing was clawing its way through the concrete, there was no blood on the walls. It was as close to comfortable as I could be. Under the circumstances.

—came shouting up out of the water like a banshee!

Yes!

There was something I could do! Almost too easy—

Wait.

Start with waiting.

Stood in the air-blaster for a long time, shaking my hair dry, and grinning, thinking, planning, calculating, weighing this against that—

Game it out and get clear on the goal, Mandy.

Don't walk in anywhere without a game plan. Playing by ear is a good way to lose an ear. Or even what's between the ears.

Stood in front of the closet a long time, debating. Look grim and serious? Or casual? Easy decision. I don't do casual. And for this visit, grim would be much more appropriate.

The other decision was harder. Normally, I don't carry. It's too dangerous. Statistics show you're much more likely to get shot if you're in the same room with a gun than if you're not in the same room.

And where I was planning to go, a gun would be more than useless, it would be a very bad idea. It would only make them angrier. Perfume would be a much deadlier weapon. Particularly one laced with musk and pheromones.

Unlocked the safe. The red bottle. Sprayed a single whiff of it into the air and walked through the whiff. That would be enough. More than enough. Even that much was dangerous.

The subway stops three blocks from The Wall. You can see it from a mile away. Behind the wall is Troll Town. The wall is seven stories high and made of crushed automobiles with concrete poured over it. The city mothers believe that this is sufficient to keep the trolls contained. They're wrong, of course, but it's a polite fiction that both trolls and humans observe—for the moment anyway. Because it's convenient.

If the trolls ever decided to take down the wall, they could do it in a matter of hours. Maybe less if they had a few tunnel trolls working it.

But the trolls are smart enough to realize that if they tore apart the city, the trainloads of beer and beef and apples and potatoes would stop rolling in. Peace was rarely bought so cheaply. Keep a troll fed and he's happy. Mostly. Trolls still have penises, impressive ones, and they like to copulate. They can do it for hours without tiring—mostly with each other.

It's quite a show—something like marathon Sumo wrestling in a vat of testosterone soup. Sometimes the foreplay battle can go on for a week or longer. The act of copulation is usually consummated in a day or two. As long as they can get drunk and fuck trolls have little urge to attack anyone or anything. Conventional wisdom has it that Troll Town is two meals and a keg away from revolution. No one wants to test this.

When they can get them, trolls also like to couple with horses, cows, pigs, anything with a hole—but horses, cows, and pigs rarely survive a troll's enthusiastic attention. In fact, it's an embarrassment to the troll if an animal does. The whole point is having "a good fuck and a snack afterward."

So it's not just dangerous for a woman to walk into Troll Town, it's a death wish. Death by orgasm. Despite the commonly held belief that trolls are sexual monsters, those who have survived have reported that their experiences were incredible. It's not that trolls are insensitive or even brutal, it's that humans lack endurance. After several hours of super-orgasm, death is inevitable.

I passed through the main gate without incident, but almost immediately a posse of smaller trolls began forming up behind me, following me at a distance, but visibly drooling. These were younglings. They wouldn't try anything, of course. The older and much larger trolls would kill them —or fuck them. Or both. And the order in which those events occurred would be up to the victor.

But no troll would approach me unless I asked him to. This was not a human rule. It was a troll rule. Otherwise, a single woman walking through the gate would trigger a deadly riot. The foreplay battles wouldn't stop until only one troll remained standing. And likely he'd be too injured to consummate. It had happened in the past, more than once, until the trolls learned to discipline their own.

Within a few minutes, I had an escort of older trolls, each one larger than the last. They hulked around me, walking slowly and methodically on their knuckles, lumbering and *whoofling* with heavy breaths and grunts. They were visibly aroused. Several stepped away to start pawing at each other. That little *whiff* of musk and pheromone was about to trigger a weekend to remember.

It was a short walk to Troll Hall. This was deliberate too. Trolls didn't want humans going very deep into Troll Town—and few humans wanted to. Inside, a single hulking oldster sat or squatted on the floor. It was hard to tell. Thick folds of sagging flesh drooped down around his haunches.

He lifted his heavy head, sniffing the air. He focused his rheumy eyes, ready to growl, then stopped when he recognized me. He blinked slowly, gathering his thoughts. Finally, his voice came like gravel in a crusty metal barrel. "What you want, Mandy?"

"I want to talk to Michael."

"He not available. He fucking."

"He's always fucking."

"True." The oldster nodded heavily. "Talk to me instead?" He sniffed the air again. "You smell good, Mandy."

"I wish I could say the same about you, Teddy. You stink like a corpse buried in three-day garbage. Don't you ever wash?"

"Would wash for you, Mandy. Give you happy ending today? You die happy."

"Thank you for the offer. If I didn't have other business, I'd be honored to accept."

"You always say that."

"So do you."

"But one day, you not have business?"

"I always have business." I said, "Like Michael."

"But you only come when Michael fucking. So you really want talk me instead."

"I can't fool you, can I?"

"You want chair?"

"That would be nice."

He shifted his huge body around, reaching for something behind him. His face contorted with the effort. He was getting old. He would not survive the next challenge to his authority.

That might happen tomorrow—or a hundred years from now. Hard to tell. Most trolls die young, from injuries inflicted in battle or injuries inflicted during copulation. Young or old, trolls die in battle, one kind or another. No troll had ever died from natural causes, so actual life expectancy was at best an educated guess. But Teddy had the advantage of size and weight, if nothing else. Fighting him would be a near-impossible challenge. Only a Tunnel troll, perhaps . . .

Finally, the old troll reached what he was grasping for and pulled a heavy chair out of some dark corner behind him. He held it up to his face and puffed heavily at it. Even from a distance I could feel the hot stink of his breath. Clouds of dust rose from the ancient cushions. He put it back down on the floor and gave it a sharp push, sliding it across the floor to me. By custom, no human ever approached within reaching distance. Also for safety reasons. Trolls are not known for their impulse control.

I sat down on the dirty chair like it was an honored throne. "Thank you, Teddy," I said. "You always treat me well."

"You bring gift?" he asked.

"No, I did not."

His expression collapsed into mottled folds of disappointment.

"But—"

He looked up, hopefully.

"—if you can help me out today, I will send

you a truckload of chocolate."

He started to shake his head. "If favor is that big, cannot." Once started, it did not seem he could stop. His huge head swiveled back and forth with a slow deliberate vigor. His jowls and his wattles were a great wrinkled sag. Thick with fat, they swung heavily with every sharp motion. "No, no, no. Even without knowing, Teddy knows. You want oath-breaking."

"Dark chocolate. The very darkest. No sugar, no sweetness at all."

"You man-bitch, Mandy."

"Yes, I am." I leaned forward. "I'm just not *your* bitch. You and I both know that a troll oath is only as good as the highest bidder. That's me. Let's bargain."

"Hmph," he said, his denials denied. "How big a truck."

"Eighteen-wheeler. Packed to the top."

"You keep your word this time?"

"Don't I always keep my word to you, Teddy?"

Teddy frowned, sorting through old memories. "Maybe you do, maybe you don't. Is always first time."

That was interesting. It was dangerous to break a promise to a troll. You wouldn't do it without good reason. A *compelling* reason. I had to ask. "Somebody broke their word to you recently?"

"Not talk about that."

"Not talk about that for how much?"

"Not talk about that for anything. We handle it ourselves."

"Okay. I won't ask." I lifted my hands in a gesture of hands-off. It was clear he'd taken that one off the table. I didn't have time to feel sorry for the whoever. I'd probably read about it in the papers if I didn't hear it from Mom first. I stared across at him, meeting his suspicious gaze. "Let's talk about that truckload of chocolate instead."

"Unwrapped? Stale?"

"Just the way you like it."

"How soon?"

"How stale do you want it?"

"Hard stale. Turned white."

"A month stale? Okay, Teddy. That's a lot. But I'll do it—if you can tell me what I want to know."

"What that?"

"Who woke up the Tunnel troll? Who pointed it at me?"

"Tunnel troll awake? When that happen?"

"Don't play dumb with me, Teddy. I know you. You know everything."

"Mandy," he looked at me woefully. It was the most mournful expression I'd ever seen on a troll. It was the face of loss and sadness and unquenchable chocolate hunger. "Not lie to you. Know nothing about tunnel troll. You say it awake?"

"Not anymore. I'm sorry."

"It dead?"

"It dead."

"You kill it?"

"Yes, I'm sorry."

"You not sorry," Teddy said. Not quite an accusation, but enough.

""Teddy. Listen careful. You and I, we know each other long time. We both see many trolls die. Too many. Not good." I let those words sink in, then added, "I not like killing. And I not like killing trolls the most. It's hard work—and very expensive."

"Yes. True. Tell me—it fight good? It die well?"

"It died hard. Very hard."

Teddy nodded, grunted. "Okay. That good." Then he smiled. "But I bet it wish to die fucking."

"Who doesn't?" But he still hadn't answered my question. "So you don't know who woke it?"

Teddy shook his head heavily. Even after he stopped, his massive jowls continued to swing like pendulums. "I not go down there, never anymore. No one go. Tunnel trolls do not fuck gentle. I show you injuries." He started to pull at the folds of flesh on his left side, attempting to reveal his own posterior. If I thought he'd smelled bad before, the waves of odor unleashed now were enough to make me wish I wasn't sitting—so I could step back. Way back. Teddy struggled with the effort for a few moments, then gave it up as a bad idea. He let go and his great rolls of skin and fat sagged back down to the floor. But the smell still lingered.

"Teddy," I said slowly. "I believe you. You

didn't answer my question, but I will send you chocolate anyway. But only a box of chocolate. Not a truckload, just a box. But hard stale chocolate. A gift of thanks." I held up my phone so he could see me punch the order in.

"You be bitch," Teddy grunted, "but a generous bitch."

I rose to go. "Just one last question. If you don't know who could wake a tunnel troll, who would know?"

Teddy looked puzzled. He furrowed his brow in concentration. Finally, he said mournfully. "Not know that either. Only person who know be person who go."

"Yes, I see. Hm. Thank you again, Teddy. That's helpful too. Very helpful. I'll send two boxes."

"You come back, see me again? When you not have business? We make big ugly baby? New king of trolls."

"I'd love to, Teddy—but if I got up and walked away afterward, wouldn't you be embarrassed?"

"It be worth it for you, Mandy."

We both laughed. His was a horrendous booming. Mine was a careful chuckle and a polite smile. Whatever else he was, Teddy was still a troll.

NINE

I was alone at one end of the subway car. There weren't many other passengers, but the few who boarded after me took one sniff and moved to the far end of the car, or even another car entirely. The stink of Troll Town was all over me. Teddy especially.

This was the first time he'd been unable to answer a question. And it wasn't that my bribe hadn't been high enough. He truly didn't know. That was scary in its own way.

I wanted to talk to Mom, and after that I'd need to see Red again. And they weren't the only ones I wanted to visit. I had a gnawing feeling in my gut that this whole thing was the prelude to another war. And the last one—yeah.

But first things first. An hour in the shower to wash the stink off. At least an hour. Whatever factors make up the awful smell of a troll, it sticks to everything. The trolls who work in civil service are required to bathe three times a day in peppermint-astringent foam and even that doesn't help much. Apparently, trolls enjoy their own smell. If that's true, they're the only ones. Trolls don't like bathing and not many are willing to bathe regularly for the privilege of working around humans. Even Mom has trouble filling out the force. If it weren't for the high pay, plus the beer and chocolate benefits, not to mention the occasional opportunity to bash a human legally, she probably wouldn't have any trolls at all working security.

Jackie wasn't happy to see me at the No-Tel Motel. "You left the room a mess."

"You mean I left it cleaner than I found it." I laid some bills on the counter anyway. "This should cover it."

"I'll call Bobo," she said.

"Thank you." I turned back to her. "Just for the record. Cleanliness is next to impossible."

"I've heard that."

"You know how they're always predicting that someday the nano-bugs will be everywhere and all those micro-signals from each one to all the ones around it and so on and so on will create a worldwide meta-web . . . ?"

"Yeah?"

"It's not a prediction anymore."

She frowned. "You mean—?"

"That's right. There's no more privacy." I scooped up the key and headed for the clean room.

It seemed obvious now. It was the only explanation for how *she* had tracked me, how the security of my sanctuary had been breached. We lived in cyber-smog. We eat it, we breathe it, we swim in it. It's us. We cannot walk down the street without nano-bugs attaching themselves to our hair, our clothes, our skin, the soles of our shoes. Decontamination is an illusion. The only immediate defense is a jam-suit. If that. But probably not. Creating a hole of darkness in the smog would be just as noticeable as wearing a bright red flashing light on your hat.

Wherever you went in the world, whatever you did, whoever you did it with, you now had to know that you were being monitored, tracked, logged, and observed by silent eyes and ears. The great mass of humanity lived lives of quiet domestication. That was the only safety—be ordinary, so ordinary you were boring. It was only when you broke out of the routine mundanities of existence that the cyber-smog would flag your activities as anomalous. That's when you attract attention. You'd leave a wake, ripples in the cyber-sea, and there are always agencies curious enough to wonder what direction those ripples revealed you to be heading.

I could retire, of course—but even that would be a break in the pattern. That would call even more attention to me. The only thing for me to do was keep doing what I would have done anyway.

Bobo joined me in the shower again. This time he just stood and kneaded my shoulders for a long, long time. I unloaded on him, the quick version of everything. *Her*. Red. Mom. The dead boy in my apartment. Sanctuary. *Her* again. The tunnel troll. Mom again. Troll Town. The death of privacy. Everything. He worked my shoulders in silence.

Finally, Bobo let his hands fall away. "Mandy, Mandy, Mandy," he whispered. "What am I going to do with you?" He pulled me back against him. I let him wrap his arms around me. I let him hold me and pretend that he was keeping me safe. "I'm serious," he said. "Stop fighting this war and marry me. I'll even let you be the girl whenever you want. I'll even grow a new penis for you."

"That's the best offer I've had all day," I sighed.

"Considering that the only other offers were *her* and an old troll, I'm not flattered."

I turned around to face him, pressing my breasts against the hard brown wall of his chest. "Bobo, if I were ever going to marry anyone, it would be you. Penis or no. But I would be the worst husband you could imagine and an even worse wife. I love you too much to do that to you."

"You think I don't know how awful a person you are?" He pulled me into an embrace and I didn't resist. "That's one of the things I love most about you."

"Bobo," I said. "If there were ever a day when I would say yes to you, today would be the day. But no—I can't let go of this one. I have to see it through to the end."

"Even if it's your end . . . ?"

"That's another reason why I can't marry you. I don't want you stuck with the funeral bill."

"Ah, but I would inherit your vast fortune, wouldn't I? Wouldn't that cover it?"

"Not quite. I want a Viking funeral. I want my body put to sea on a flaming boat—the biggest one in the harbor."

"That one?" he asked.

"Yes, *that* one," I confirmed. "After you pay for that, there will be nothing left but my unpaid bar tabs. That will bankrupt you. No, I love you too much for that."

"And if not me, then it'll be a half-dozen bars declaring bankruptcy if those debts go into default."

"If I go down," I sighed, "the economy goes down with me."

"Speaking of going down . . ." he offered. He took my hand and led me to the bed. He was very convincing.

Later, drifting in the afterglow, staring at the ceiling, pondering that strange unidentifiable stain shaped like Idaho, I began to wonder if perhaps Bobo might be right. There was only one of me. There were an awful lot of them. The universe had me outnumbered. Ohell, the universe has all of us outnumbered. What's the point of fighting back anyway. Death is still inevitable. Why not just relax and enjoy what's left of the ride?

"What are you thinking?" Bobo asked.

"I'm thinking maybe a smaller boat for the funeral. There's no need to be gaudy."

"Actually, I was planning to keep the money and bury you in the garden. Under the rose bushes, I think. They're looking a little tired."

"Thoughtful, very thoughtful."

He rolled over onto his side to face me, placing a hand gently on my belly. "Seriously, Mandy. I'm worried for you. No—" He corrected himself. "I'm terrified for you."

I rolled to face him. "Bobo—"

He placed a finger across my lips. "Don't say it. I'm really tired of hearing you say no. It's time for you to start thinking yes."

"Bobo—" And this time, I put two fingers on his mouth to keep him from speaking. "The moment I say yes to anyone, I put that person in danger. I can't do that. I have to keep my distance. Physically. Emotionally. I couldn't stand it if I lost you."

His eyes narrowed. Hurt.

"Can you live with that? Can't we just have what we have?"

After a moment, he blinked and gave me a half-nod. He met my eyes with a shiny glance. "Can you at least say that this will be your last job?"

"You know I can't say that." I took a deep breath. "The minute I stop moving, I'm a target. And everyone around me. You're already in enough danger. I don't want to make it worse."

He sat up in bed, bracing himself with his

hands, half frozen in the act of getting up. He stared at the opposite wall for a long moment. He stared *past* the opposite wall as if looking deep into tomorrow. "That's not good enough," he said it with finality and rolled himself out of bed. "I think I'm done." He padded into the bathroom.

"Shit," I said, sitting up. I rolled out of bed after him.

He was sitting on the toilet, tinkling into the bowl. I looked at him. He looked sadly back at me. He shook his head. "You're never going to find another man who will go down on you while you still stink of Troll Town."

"That's true."

"You're going to die old and alone. You know that, don't you?"

"Alone, probably. Old? The odds are very much against it."

He didn't like that answer. He finished. He stood. He flushed the toilet and stepped into the shower. It came on automatically. "There's a clean dress for you hanging in the closet," he called over the splashing. It was a dismissal. I ignored it and stepped into the shower after him. He turned away from me—so I grabbed the soap and started washing his back. It was my turn to work on the tension in his neck and shoulders. I could feel the anger in his muscles.

"This is about *her*, isn't it?" he said.

"Absolutely not."

"I see the look on your face when you talk

about *her.* I hear the shift in your voice. You still love her."

"No, I don't."

"Okay. You love her memory."

"No. Not even that."

"Then what is it?"

"Bobo—" I said. "It's so hard. I—I can't forgive her. I keep trying. But I can't." I stopped kneading his shoulders for a moment. "I want her to leave me alone, but she won't."

"And—?"

"And the truth is, every time she comes back, I want to hurt her. So hard you can't imagine. As hard as she hurt me. No, harder than that." After a moment more, I added, "Yeah, I know that's not possible. I think that's why I want to do it. The frustration. There's just no way to resolve it."

"You're not the only one who's frustrated," he said.

"I'm sorry, Bobo. If it's any consolation, I'm truly sorry."

"No, you don't have to apologize. I understand. Maybe better than you. You just can't let go of her. You say you can, but you won't."

"You make it sound so—"

"Because that's how it is."

I had no answer for that. He stepped out of the shower, leaving me alone in the stinging spray. I slapped it off and stood there, steam rising all around me.

"Shit!" I said it loudly.

"You said a mouthful," he called from the other room.

TEN

When I finally stepped out of the shower, Bobo was gone and I was alone again.

I had hoped he would understand. That he had read between the lines. Maybe he had. Maybe his angry exit had actually been a performance for anyone watching. But also—maybe he hadn't understood what I couldn't say aloud. And if that were true, then he'd meant every word of his good-bye. And maybe I really was alone.

But at least I wasn't dead. Not yet.

And I still had no idea what any of this was about. It wasn't about the murders. It never had been. It was about something else, something so well hidden it was beyond invisible. Something so powerful it could kill a Silver, put a headless body in my bathtub, reveal a Class-Nine Sanctuary, and awaken a tunnel troll.

The troll was the key. More so now that Teddy had no clue who had awakened it. This wasn't troll business, and that was something else useful to know.

The sun was already dipping beneath the western horizon when I stepped out of the motel room. The evening glowed orange beneath glowering thunderheads. The rain was scheduled to begin just before midnight, but a dark wind was already rising. I pulled my cloak close around me.

Phoned for my car and waited patiently for it to pull up in front of the motel. It was certainly still bugged, but now that I knew the impossibility of secrecy, it didn't matter anymore. The only other possibility was to be such an annoyance that my hidden adversaries were forced to reveal themselves. If you're going to shake the tree, shake it loud and shake it hard.

My destination wasn't far, but the car had to cross through a wide tract of abandoned buildings. Demolition teams had not yet finished their work and the car had to steer carefully around wide piles of bricks and rubble. By the time I arrived, most of the remaining streetlights had come on.

This was not one of the happier parts of the city. The storefronts glittered with cheap displays. The apartment windows above revealed shabby furnishings within, faded lamps and dreary curtains. Despite the easy availability of better lodgings elsewhere, empty and spacious, there were still many who preferred their cramped little neighborhoods.

A shadowed corner of the boulevard—a second glance revealed a subdued purple glow, a dark invitation, almost unnoticeable at the end of a long row of blackened storefronts. No identifying sign. If you didn't already know it was there, you weren't welcome. A gathering place for those seeking the delusion of privacy.

And even if you did know it was there, you couldn't assume an invitation. The Meet Rack catered to the half-men and the men who followed them, another community of the night—by choice more than necessity. Fantasies bloom brighter in darkness. They would gather here before heading out to the nests of their Queens.

Silence as I entered. Slim bodies clustered. Hopeful faces turned, then turned away quickly. I ignored it all and strode to the back. Dark velvet walls, dark leather booths. Hangings outlined imaginary spaces in a red and purple world. Wall sconces simulated open flames, they cast flickering shadows. Everything wrapped itself in the illusion of ancient sorceries.

He was sitting in his usual booth, quietly conversing with another halfling. They both looked up at the same time. I had obviously interrupted something important, but he nodded to the other and the halfling slid out and faded quickly into darkness.

"Mandy." He nodded.

"Hello, Trent. Mind if I sit?" I didn't wait for his answer. I slipped into the seat opposite. It was still warm, almost hot. Halflings have a higher body temperature than humans.

"You have a lot of nerve coming in here."

"The door opened for me."

"You still have a lot of nerve."

"If you feel that way, then why did you have the door pass me in?"

"Because I've been expecting you. Any time there's trouble with her, there you are. And after that, here you are."

"I need your help."

"Yes, you do."

"You know my situation?"

"Don't I always?"

"Maybe not this time."

"You went with her."

"I listened."

Trent waited for me to explain. I chose not to.

Finally, he said, "Everyone saw you go. So it doesn't matter what she said or what you heard. Everyone knows you're connected. Somehow. So, you want to fill me in?"

"I'm being used."

"I just said that."

"I want to know by who."

"Can't help you there." He regarded his drink warily. "Even if I knew anything—"

"Yeah, right. You can't put yourself at risk either. Just the same, now that I'm here—everybody knows I'm here, knows I'm talking to you, so it doesn't matter what you tell me."

Trent nodded. "You'll do whatever you're going to do, Mandy. Whatever it is. You always do." He finished his drink, then looked across at me. "But this time, you're going alone. I won't be part of it." He held up his empty glass and waggled it at a passing waiter for a refill. "You'll go alone and whoever's watching you—what you'll do next, that's on you. No one else."

"Even that tells me something. It tells me that you're scared."

"If that's what you want to believe, sure. Over here, it's just not cost-effective. There's no appreciable benefit for me. For us." He waved his hand to indicate the larger community of half-men. "It's nothing we need to be a part of."

"Hm. An interesting position. But I wonder if the Queens would agree with you. If someone or something is arousing the tunnel trolls, they might have a different feeling about need-to-know."

Trent stopped. He put his glass down. He stared at me, a flash of anger in his eyes. "You want to ask them?"

"That's why I'm here."

He waited for me to explain. I leaned forward and spoke as sincerely as I could. "Trent, something has happened. Is still happening. Something very big."

"Something you can't tell me?"

"Something I can't uncover by myself. I don't ask easily, you know that. I need your help."

"And you want me to trust you? Again?" he asked, his anger edging cautiously toward curiosity.

The serving boy replaced Trent's empty glass with a full one. I waited until he was gone. "A Silver has died."

Trent shook his head. "We would have heard."

"Murdered."

His eyes widened. "How do you know this?"

"A Silver told me. No one else knows."

"Why would a Silver confide in you?"

"Because he did."

He sniffed skeptically, but I had his attention now.

"I don't think it's the first murder. I think there've been others. Perhaps a decade ago. Maybe longer. There are Silvers who have disappeared from public view."

"That doesn't mean anything. They can go years without being seen. There are probably some we haven't seen for centuries, maybe some we've never known."

"True enough. But think on this. If a Silver can be murdered, how safe are your Queens?"

He shrugged. "It's irrelevant. The Silvers have their own affairs. We have ours."

"Are you certain of that? Do the Queens think the same way?"

He didn't answer.

The First Transformations had revealed

the Silvers to the world. Later, the second and third waves had brought forth trolls and halfling Queens—and a few other things, less discussed. All the *Changes* were of a kind, linked in ways still unknown—and even among those transformed, none were certain that the times of *Change* were fully passed. Anything that threatened the well-being of one race might very well represent a danger to the others.

The Silvers were playing a long game, they wouldn't acknowledge any threat as immediate. The trolls would bluster at it, puffing themselves up and beating their chests in displays of defiance. But the halfling Queens—they would stop and consider the possibilities, all the immediate ramifications and long-term consequences. The Queens would understand enough to be scared.

And Trent—the highest-ranking halfling in the district—would have to know that.

"What do you want?" he asked.

"Twelve halfling commandos. Equipped for spelunking. With at least six fully charged dazzlers."

To his credit, Trent didn't flinch.

"When?"

"As soon as possible?"

"I'll have to make a call. Wait here." He slid out of the booth, disappeared into the back.

The half-men had no reason to trust me. Considering everything that had happened in the past, their skepticism was more than justified. Our previous encounters had not ended well. Plenty of blame for everyone, but myself in particular. I had made a mistake and half-men had died. Even worse, they'd died at the hands of a lust-enraged troll.

And now I was asking for a chance to repeat that mistake.

A pale boy slid into the booth opposite me. Dressed all in black. A half-man wannabe? He looked familiar, but I couldn't place him. "You shouldn't be here," he said.

ELEVEN

I did that thing I do when people threaten me —either obliquely or directly.

I stared blankly into his face.

And waited.

And then I recognized him.

It was Laz. The boy from the keep.

He was probably augmented. Everybody is now, especially everybody who deals with Silvers. He'd probably read my reaction, even before I finished reacting. Well, good. He should know that I recognized him—and that whatever he said, it would be another piece of the puzzle. Another move in the game.

Laz got uncomfortable waiting for me to say something. Finally, he just repeated. "You shouldn't be here."

So I waited some more.

He wanted me to ask why, so he could tell me I was in danger.

Instead, I studied him. He was beautiful in

his own ethereal way. And he had something else —ah, I could see it now. He had an artificially enhanced charisma. Not overwhelming, but enough to unbalance the emotions of the unwary.

"You need to leave. Now."

"Okay, why—?"

"Because Red needs you alive. For now, anyway. Don't be stupid. They're going to kill you—"

"Who?"

But Laz was already gone. He'd slipped out of the booth and vanished into the shadows. If he was wearing a dark cloak—and who wasn't these days—then he'd already flipped it and *was* a shadow, an unresolvable blur of deeper-than-velvet black. The darker dark in the dark.

Did I believe him?

Or had Red sent him to stop me from investigating?

I wasn't supposed to investigate anyway— just be a decoy.

But how could I be a decoy if I didn't investigate?

And if someone was tracking me, whoever was tracking me, they wouldn't know I was a decoy. But they wouldn't believe I was important if I didn't investigate something.

I knew what the problem was.

The chessboard was too big for me to see all the way to the horizon.

Too many pieces in play.

Too many variables.

Too many queens.

And suddenly, I was a key piece. Even as a feint, a distraction, I was important.

The hell with this. I'm not a player in this tournament and I didn't ask to be a piece. Fuck it.

Discretion being the better part of survival, I flipped my own dark cloak and headed for the door.

I almost made it.

Someone or something grabbed for my arm, but the dark cloak makes resolution impossible, whatever it was missed—

It followed me out the door, but then it took off running in the opposite direction—

I was already fading into the nearest shadow, stunner sliding out of my sleeve, but even as I turned to face the non-attacker, something slammed me backward—

The Meet Rack exploded.

The discreet little door burst outward in a gout of flame, the building expanded as if suddenly inflated, and then walls and roof shattered outward. Three separate shockwaves. Boom-flash-boom. Nicely done. No survivors. No one to gossip.

And if the ever-present snoops hadn't offloaded what they'd seen, there would be nothing significant for anyone to see, nothing to speculate about.

I picked myself up, checked for damage, no more than usual. My readouts were their usual flickering yellow. Not surprising. My check-engine light was permanently on. Occupational hazard. If you could call this an occupation.

Options. Best one? Leave.

Summoned my car, hesitated—what if it had been tampered with too? But its confidence was high—

—but before it arrived, a dark blur stepped up next to me. It slid its hood back.

"Spare a ride?" It was Laz.

"Where's yours?"

"We should talk."

My car arrived, the door slid open. "All right."

He slid in after me, taking the seat opposite.

"Home," I told the car. I looked across at him. "You can find your way from there?"

"Won't be a problem."

I studied him. He had the glow of a whatever. Still unchosen, but already positioning for possibility. Whatever was offered. And he was beautiful. Eminently fuckable too. No, I wouldn't push him out of bed for eating crackers.

It was a strange thing to consider—considering the circumstances.

Maybe I was in shock. Narrowly escaping death can do that to a mind. I felt my emotional overrides kicking in, damping my autonomics until it was safe for me to react. Otherwise, I would have trembled in shock, but no—my system shifted automatically to passive-aggressive.

Because I was just too tired to care anymore.

Whatever.

If someone wants to kill me, obviously I'm not that hard to find.

And if someone else wants to keep me from being killed, I shouldn't make their job harder either.

I took him home.

I was tired. I needed to get some sleep. But I needed answers more. If not answers, then information. Anything.

I'd be hearing from Mom soon enough. And probably Red as well. And anyone else who wanted to intrude on my time—and without paying for it either. Probably some surviving half-men and maybe a curious troll, probably a few whatevers as well. They would all have as many questions as I had, none of them answerable.

But at least, I had Laz. "You said we need to talk?"

He shook his head. "Not in the car."

"Why not?"

He shook his head a second time. "Invite me in. Coffee? A drink?"

"A fuck?"

He half-shrugged, half-smiled. Not quite an invitation, but not quite a rejection either. A possibility, maybe.

"Let's just have coffee."

The house was dark. But just the same, I entered first, stunner in hand. Laz waited at the door.

I checked my bathtub and my refrigerator.

They were clean. Thanks Bobo.

But I still had no intention of using either—not in the foreseeable future.

Turned out, I was out of coffee. I'd been out of coffee for three and a half years. "You want a beer?"

"You don't have any. Not here anyway."

"Really? You know that?"

Laz shrugged, smiled, spread his hands wide and half-nodded in a bow of admission.

I wasn't fooled.

All right, a drink instead.

The second drawer of the desk—

"No, not that," said Laz. "The good stuff, please." He pointed at a terrible old picture on the wall. "I'm worth it," he said.

"You'd better be—" I took the picture down. Behind it was a hole in the plaster. And a square bottle. It looked black, but in bright daylight it would reveal a blue so deep as to strain the ability of a normal retina to resolve.

I found a couple of shot glasses, rinsed them in the sink, shook them dry, put them on the kitchen table. Sat down. Poured two shots. Waited for Laz to sit down opposite me.

He lifted his glass, sniffed, looked across it to me. "What are we drinking to?"

"Let's drink to honesty, a rare commodity in this town."

"In this world." He raised his glass in salute, sniffed again, smiled, sipped, smiled even wider.

"Yes, very nice."

"You're not as innocent as you look."

"No one is," he said. "At least, no one we know."

"There's that."

"You still miss her," he said. It wasn't a question.

"That's what everyone thinks. I'm not going to argue."

"You got in the car."

"Curiosity," I said. It was a lie and we both knew it. "My turn to ask questions. Does Red know you're here?"

Laz nodded. "Probably."

"He sent you?"

"No."

"But you assume he knows."

"You said it yourself. In Mom's office. There are no secrets anymore."

"That's not quite true. It's a secret if you don't tell anyone."

"Possibly. It all depends on how good they are at reading patterns."

"And reading minds?"

"Hard to do without grabbing you and putting a headset on you—and even then, all you have to do is sing a song to yourself. That usually confuses the monitors. So—" He took another drink.

"So," I said. "If Red doesn't know you're here —no, check that—if Red didn't send you, then why are you here? No, check that too. Who are you really working for?"

He shrugged. "Damfino."

"But Red knows you're spying on him?"

"Uh-huh. That's why he keeps me close. So he can feed specific information to whoever hired me."

"But you don't know who?"

Laz grinned. "I'm just a poor boy, from a poor family—"

"You do know how that song ends . . . ?"

Laz stopped smiling. "I was offered a job. I accepted. Someone paid for my enhancements. Every so often, I get instructions. Like tonight. Whenever convenient, I upload. I don't ask questions. I have a better life than before. I eat well. I wear nice clothes. And I'm pretty. Yes, I was bought and paid for. And no, I don't have any regrets. It's a good life—"

"If it lasts."

"Timing," said Laz. He reached for the bottle. "Like tonight. It's all about timing."

"Okay, so . . ." I poured myself a second drink. "I assume there's nothing else you need from me—except my liquor. So tell me what you want me to know."

"You haven't figured it out yet?"

"I haven't figured out anything. Have you?"

"No."

"And that's what you want me to know?"

"No. What I want you to know—" He hesitated. "There are more players in this game than

133

either you or I will ever know. What I want you to know is who I am—"

"Except you don't even know who you are, do you?"

"No, but now you know as much as I do."

I thought about it. He waited patiently. Finally, I said, "Well, I'm going to assume. rightly or wrongly, that whoever you belong to—really belong to—is someone with a lot of money, a lot of power, and a lot of ability to data mine the web. We already know how good they are at tracking. So my first guess would be the billie-boys."

"That's been my assumption. But they operate through untraceable go-betweens, so it could be anybody."

"Right. But—let me extrapolate something. Several somethings. They, whoever they might be, don't want me talking to any of the queens. That's immediately obvious. Second, they are assuming I know something they don't and they want to know what it is, so that's why they had you save my life."

Laz spread his hands—surrender. "I only know that I was told to go there and warn you."

"You said *they* were going to kill me. Which *they*?"

"I wasn't told that either. Just told to warn you."

"I suppose I should appreciate it."

Laz unbuttoned his cloak and let it fall onto the back of the chair. His shirt was shining black

—some variation of silk. The top was slightly open, revealing his pale milk-white skin. For some reason, I thought of the headless body in the bathtub.

"Do you have siblings?"

Laz shook his head. "No. And I know what you're thinking. No, I'm not a clone. I'm remodeled. Not a public pattern."

"Yes, of course. And that is interesting. Who owns the pattern?"

Laz shook his head. "Don't know that either."

"Hm. Maybe whoever killed that boy was really after you—? And got the wrong one?"

Laz considered pouring himself a third drink. Instead, he pushed the shot glass away. "Yeah, Red considered that. He told me."

"Aren't you scared?"

"I'm not wired for fear. I don't miss it."

"Pity. It can be useful." Another thought. "What *are* you wired for?"

"I can tell you—or I can show you."

I studied him. He was beautiful. What the fuck, why not?

We both stood up at the same time. His shirt opened at my touch and I traced the smoothness of his naked chest with my fingers. He wasn't Bobo, but he was . . . interesting. I hadn't done it with a girl-boy in a long time.

And yes—it was sweet, it was fun—and in another life, maybe we could have been something. But right now, we were just—whatever we were.

Maybe that's all he needed me to know. Just that.

TWELVE

I slept badly.

My head was full of dreams. *She* was there, of course. I was chasing her down a darkened city street—it bordered a walled-in park, a sanctuary of some kind, maybe she was running for the gate, but there was no gate. Her clothes were white bandages, tattered and falling off her as she ran. She ran into the street, momentarily confused, then she ran back to the sidewalk, back the way she came—right into the pursuing death squad—men and women in black leather uniforms and black sunglasses. The woman was young and athletic, she had her hair pulled back, she had bright red lipstick, and she was smiling wide enough to reveal bright white teeth. And fangs? Sunglasses at night? Why was it so bright? The death squad ambushed both of us. They shot her first and then me. I woke up shaking—

Took a few seconds to realize I was awake. And shuddering. An after-shock from the explosion of the Meet Rack? Or maybe just a wake-up quake.

A hand on my arm—Laz. Tousled but still beautiful. Whoever designed that pattern, that was a first-class remodel. "Are you all right?" he asked.

I didn't answer. I blinked my eyes to clarity. The glow on the ceiling said four-thirty in the ayem. A little too early for dawn, a little too late for anything else. Well, not quite. Laz was still here. And he was still beautiful.

I pulled him close. He didn't resist. Instead —if that wasn't genuine enthusiasm, then he was one hell of a performer. Either way, a pleasant surprise.

Afterward, I drifted back to a much more satisfying sleep. I wondered if Red would let me borrow Laz for a few years—

There are a lot of different ways to think about sex. For some people, it's about power over other people. I've had a few of those encounters. I let two of them live, but not undamaged. I have no patience with that particular brand of selfishness.

For others, sex is just exercise, a momentary bit of pleasure. I have no problem with that, but neither do I have any desire to pursue it. I might occasionally indulge, but at its best, it's a convenience, not a career.

At its best, sex is a physical conversation between two bodies. Augmented, it's a shared consciousness inhabiting two bodies simultaneously, but that usually requires linked augments—and that's not for the squeamish. It's a skill.

But when the physical conversation works —and when it works so well that consciousness dissolves in connection—it's nirvana, coming back from the far side.

Laz was very good. Almost perfect. I wouldn't expect less from a remodel. The physical conversation was eloquent, elegant, and inspiring. Almost perfect—

—but *she* had been perfect without a remodel, without the augments, without the enhancements.

It's probably not fair for me to compare one with the other. And it's probably not accurate either. Memory plays tricks. I've been told that addiction is caused by the memory of pleasure, the attempt to recapture the initial rush of amazement and wonder. Okay, that might explain sex-addiction, but does it also explain—?

Never mind.

I'll take what I can get. I'll get what I can take.

Bobo is fun, thoughtful, generous. Laz is exquisite and delicious. Chocolate and strawberry. Different flavors. But neither are that flavor that I will never have again and still miss.

I realized I was awake. Staring at the ceiling.

And a bizarre thought was circling in my head. It didn't make sense—except it almost did. Something about chess players.

But what the hell—at this point, any idea was possible. I added it to the list of improbables, right behind Colonel Mustard in the Conservatory with the flamethrower.

Laz was sleeping peacefully beside me. I wasn't going to wake him. Not yet. If I did, he'd smile—and I'd be tempted for another round of whatever I could have. I was pretty sure he wouldn't say no.

Maybe I'd ask him why. "What do you see in me?"

If he was honest, he'd probably say, "Nothing at all. It's just my job."

That was not an answer I wanted to hear. So, for the moment, I'd pretend that the physical conversation was also an expression of connection.

Meanwhile . . .

I had to assume that I no longer had any friends in this town. I hadn't had any to begin with, hadn't had any since *she* took the shine. Word around town had it that I had turned into a bitter, angry, drunk. Not true. I hadn't turned into one. I had always been bitter and angry. And the drinking was just a way to make sure I wouldn't end up with too much blood in my alcohol stream.

Not sure what my next move might be.

Too many unanswered questions.

Who blew up the Meet Rack? And why?

Somebody wanted to make a point—but what point?

And why was it important? Wouldn't it have

been better to just let me flail around for a while?

Unless the point was to remove a piece from the board—

Because the other player thought the piece was important? The game was apparently more a series of skirmishes than an all-out assault. Except that some of those skirmishes were deadly, especially for the smalls.

If the smalls had any idea how they were being played—

They would play back, wouldn't they?

What would their move be?

Somebody blew up the Meet Rack.

And somebody else knew about it.

Far enough in advance to send Laz to warn me.

Unless Laz had been tracking me the whole time—sent by Red? Warned by whoever?

Maybe the club was supposed to blow up anyway, whether I was there or not? Which implied a whole other set of possibilities—that there were even more parts of this game than just murdering the occasional Silver. Maybe the halflings were a target too, Trent anyway.

I'd have to find out if he survived. Where did he disappear to? Did he leave the building because he knew what was about to happen—

Did Trent blow up the club—and half his regular clientele? Or did someone else do it to take out both of us? Or just for the hell of it?

If the former, then Trent knew a lot more

than he'd admitted. If the latter, then someone was watching Trent as closely as they were watching me—which meant that Trent wasn't going to be allowed to find out anything. All of which meant that there was something to find out.

The only thing for sure—if nothing else, it was a pointer toward something. Or away from something.

It was information. Like a single piece of a jigsaw puzzle is information. But without more pieces, you have no idea where it fits or what the entire picture might be.

I had a theory, one of several. One of many.

I'd have to think about them each in turn.

There was something in the tunnel. Something going on with the trolls, perhaps? Something that had awakened them.

Something that had resulted in the death of a Silver?

Considering everything, that was the most logical.

Which was why it was probably wrong.

Wait—

Maybe it hadn't been a human who'd killed a Silver.

Maybe it had been a troll.

That raised an interesting question. Could a troll kill a Silver?

If that were true, then that would be something that the Silvers wouldn't want anyone to know—especially trolls. It could start a war. It would definitely upset the balance of power.

Follow that thought.

Somebody needs something from down in the tunnels.

Maybe they woke up a troll.

And got killed.

And now the trolls are muttering around under the city.

But where do the Silvers come in?

Unless it was a Silver who was poking around—

—and somebody else woke up a troll to stop that Silver.

So who would want to wake up a troll?

Somebody who knew what the Silver was looking for—and didn't want them to find it.

Because they were looking for it themselves?

Which eventually circles back to last night's question.

If Trent didn't blow the club, then who would stand to benefit from his death?

Laz knew enough to warn me. But maybe he didn't know anything more than he was supposed to know. The Queen doesn't confide in the pawn, especially when she sends it out as a sacrifice.

Or any other piece.

We're the smalls—and we're disposable.

Hm.

I'm thinking about this as if it's a game.

Fair enough. It is.

For the people playing in it, anyway.

Not for us smalls.

But what I don't know—still haven't figured out—the thing that Red never addressed—*who's the other player?*

I've been assuming it's the billie-boys—not just the ordinary billionaires we follow in the media, but the billionaires we don't know about— the ones who buy and sell governments. They had to be players in this game—

But they might not be the only ones.

That was the other unanswered question. How many players were in this game?

Too many pieces in this puzzle.

Too many players.

If it's a Long Game, then the only other players would be Silvers. Nobody else would have the endurance. Or even the desire. Why play a game you won't live long enough to win?

So who's on the other side of the table? Insane Silvers? Why do I keep coming back to that?

And another thought.

How did Laz know where to find me?

That meant Red was not only tracking me, but actively working to keep me alive—

Because—?

Hmm.

—I was still valuable to him, somehow.

Probably because *she* wanted me kept alive.

In some vain hope that someday I would—?

Wait.

It can't be Silvers—insane or otherwise.

Because—Silvers can't kill Silvers.

But—this is the question—can Silvers hire humans or trolls or half-men to kill Silvers?

Probably, but they'd have to be marginally insane just to do that. The thought would be abhorrent.

Unless, maybe—

Now, that's interesting.

What if a Silver could sublimate the thought so deeply that he wasn't thinking about killing—he was just removing an opposing piece from the game board.

Still insane, but not as much.

Okay, follow that thought.

Silvers can't kill Silvers, but Silvers can use humans to kill other Silvers, right? You wouldn't use trolls, because you don't want trolls to know that it's possible to kill Silvers. That would be changing the abilities and motives of pieces already on the board. You don't use half-men either. You have to use humans, because humans are the most easily disposable.

Okay, so—

If you're a Silver and you know that some other Silver has figured out how to kill you, what do you do?

You hire some other humans to kill the Silvers who are hiring humans to kill Silvers.

So, here we were—on a giant chessboard, an unknown number of grandmasters jockeying for position, a scattering of pigeons strutting around, knocking over pieces, and maybe a troll or two ready to upend the whole board.

So . . .

I'm in a war.

And I don't even know which side I'm on.

It's worse than that.

It doesn't matter.

Because I don't care who's playing or even who's winning.

I just want out of the game.

THIRTEEN

By the time I got to that station in my train
of thought, dawn was already nagging at
the window. And Laz was up on one elbow
watching me.

"Shower?" he asked. An invitation.

He didn't have to ask twice.

I didn't leap out of bed, but I didn't dawdle
much either.

The chance to examine his body in the daylight was interesting. I didn't discover anything
I hadn't found out by Braille last night, but the
visual inspection had its high points, and a couple
of down-low points as well.

And a very curious thought occurred to me.

What if Red was the original model for this
pattern?

But if that were true, then why would Red
create a duplicate for the sole purpose of spying on
himself?

Unless—

No, that was just too baroque.

But if you're playing a long game with lots of shadows, you might want a few double-agents. So maybe Red had a doppelganger among the billie-boys, so that when his shadow reported what his spy had discovered, that would buy credibility —and the other side might be careless enough to share their thinking in return.

Well, it kinda made sense.

It was just hard to imagine that Red had once looked like Laz—or worse, that Laz might someday look like Red. Not that Red was unhandsome, in his own corpulent way. He just didn't have that same ethereal quality. If he ever had.

Soaping up Laz, rinsing him off for the third or fourth time, I was struck by a memory of adolescence—one of those formative incidents, that at the moment seems important, but when viewed through the telescope of memory, is just another whatever.

Laz was too beautiful to be real. That was the thing.

He reminded me of someone I had known only peripherally. It was that strange period between childhood and what passes for the first glimmers of sentience—that time when we're supposed to construct an adult identity, that part of life where a person discovers his ability to be truly depressed and unhappy.

In my case, it was a Pandora's box of existential questions. "Why me?" "Why was *I* born and not someone else?" "Why am I here?" all of which eventually morphed into: "Why couldn't I have been born to a rich family?" "Why am I in this body and not a beautiful body?" "Why am I this way and not that way?" All of which made for a cocktail of envy, a desire to be like those who were so perfect they had no problems. Because they were pretty. I wasn't bad, but I wasn't extraordinary.

And every so often, I would fixate—call it a crush—on someone who seemed so perfect to me that I wished I could be that person. Laz reminded me of one of those. Another redheaded boy, so pretty beautiful that if I couldn't be him, then at least I wanted to take him to bed. That would be a validation that if I wasn't beautiful I was at least desirable.

It was a very shallow set of desires because I was a very shallow person. There was a boy—

But eventually, I gave up and just wallowed in my life, focusing on anything that didn't involve dealing with other people. I got very good at a few things—good enough to be paid for it.

Later, though—much later—when I checked back into the world, and I saw what some of those beautiful people had turned into, I started to suspect I might have dodged a bullet. Even the prettiest get old. They get those tiny wrinkles in the soul, that slightly worn-out expression. And when they speak, they reveal the damage, the erosion of innocence, the sad slow slide into irrelevance. When life is too easy, when you get used to everyone around you fawning and favoring, you become unable to deal with even the easiest of adversities.

I saw that boy again—once. He didn't see me, or even recognize me—but he was just one more piece of meat hanging on the rack, waiting in quiet desperation for a life he'd already abandoned.

No, it didn't make me feel better. It made me even more depressed. Because the lesson there was that even the beautiful, the popular, the ones who seemingly have everything going for them—even they can't make it.

So now I had a different reason to wallow. But at least, I knew how to do that. That was the one advantage I had over all the so-called beautiful people.

And then, for no reason I could ever figure out, *she* came along—

And *she* loved me.

Where previously the world had been muddy, now it was bright. Life sparkled. Where there had been only noise, now I heard music. We laughed together. We shared the little discoveries and the big ones. We explored each other and learned about ourselves. She taught me how to fly.

At first it was only infatuation. I didn't understand why she was attracted to me—but later on, one night, she said, "It's your confidence, your strength, your solidity. Nothing can hurt you. I want to be like you—and if I can't be like you, then I want to be sheltered by your wings."

"I promise," I said. "I will always—"

"I know," she said. "That's your weakness."

But she loved me, anyway.

—Until one day, she didn't.

"What are you thinking about?" asked Laz.

"Nothing, really." I handed him a towel. "I was thinking about how beautiful you are."

"Thank you."

"No, don't thank me. It wasn't a compliment." I grabbed a towel for myself. "Beauty is bad luck. It's a curse. It makes life too easy. It spoils you. It ruins your ability to—"

"You forget who I am," he said. "I'm a re-model. I know what I was before."

"And you chose this?"

"It was easier than dying," he said.

I didn't have an answer for that. He might have been right.

FOURTEEN

Eventually, Laz slipped out.

A while after that, he said, "I gotta go."

Leaving me alone with my thoughts again.

It had been fun, but fun is just another interruption from the pain of getting from one moment to the next. Yeah, I am bitter.

He did ask me though. "Were you ever tempted?"

I hesitated before answering. What the hell, why not tell the truth? "Yeah, I admitted. I was tempted. I've also been tempted to suck the bullet out of a gun, leap off a tall building, and drink myself to death. That last one—that would take longer, but so far, I dunno, maybe I still have that one last curse, hope trapped in the box. Does that answer your question?"

He didn't smile, he didn't look shocked either. If he was everything he said he was, he probably knew the answer already. And if he didn't

THE GIRL WHO WAS SILVER

know the answer, then that might have been the whole purpose of his visit. It wasn't unplanned, nothing is accidental, there are no coincidences.

Someone always wants something. It's a condition of life.

I still didn't know who wanted it this time or what they wanted or if they got anything at all, but at least this was a nice way to ask.

It was a pleasant night. I wouldn't say no to an encore.

But inevitably, in the bleary light of unwelcome morning, the unpleasant slide back to what some people call reality. Meanwhile, no matter what happens, there I am, inside my own head.

He left and I sat alone at the table, letting my coffee get cold while I continued sorting through the questions I had and all the facts that didn't answer them.

There were possibilities, lots of possibilities, but no evidence for any of them. I took a cold sip and waited for the expected interruption. It was not long in arriving. The knock on the door was not polite. A summons from Mom.

She did not look happy.

Well, she never looks happy, but this was several degrees beyond never. "What is wrong with you, Mandy? Are you trying to destroy what's left of this city?"

I shrugged. "It might be an improvement."

Mom ignored my comment. She waited till the tremor stopped. It was barely noticeable, but every so often it wasn't. "Let's see," she began. "There's a dead boy in your apartment, that's bad enough. But at least we can handle that. We have procedures. But that's not enough for you, is it? You had to kill a tunnel troll. They're supposed to stay deep, but no, you had to wake one up. And it wasn't enough to kill the tunnel troll, you had to collapse the entire tunnel. You destroyed the connections between the Gold, Red, and Green lines."

"Sorry," I mumbled.

"Sorry is not a fucking eraser," said Mom. "Then, you doused yourself in pheromones and went to Troll Town."

"I needed information."

"You didn't consider the consequences, did you? Your little walkthrough—I'm not sure how to describe it. Riot? Orgy? Massacre? Clusterfuck? We had to seal off the whole area and hope that the quarantine holds. It should. But by the time the last one of those . . . those creatures has exhausted itself, the death toll will be . . . I don't know, nobody wants to predict. Aside from the economic effects —do you know how much this city's economy depends on troll labor? They're cheap. They're happy with potatoes, coal, and the occasional carrot. We'll be a month without a cheap source of labor, maybe two. You just pushed this entire state into a recession. And that's not even the worst of it—"

I tried to meet her gaze. It was important that I not look at my hands or my feet. She'd interpret it as shame.

"We're going to have a hundred dead trolls when this is over, maybe more. Have you ever smelled a dead troll? Do you know that dead trolls don't decompose? No self-respecting microbe on this planet wants to try. The bodies have to be shipped out to the desert. You ever visit Troll Mountain? Can't burn the bodies either. The cloud is toxic. And the whole thing has to be tarped in case of rain, the runoff is poisonous. This city can't afford the maintenance. Taxes are already back-breaking."

"Um, aren't trolls—I mean, don't they eat their dead?"

"Well, they would, yes. Under ordinary cir-cumstances. But right now, they'd rather have po-tatoes and coal and carrots. And you had to go and deliver chocolate to the troll king. We were waiting for him to die. You bought him another decade at least."

"Is there coffee?" I asked, I looked around for — "Oh, right."

"He won't be coming back," Mom said. "Too small to survive. He'll probably be one of the first fatalities. Do you know how hard it was to train him?"

"Um, yeah. Sorry about that."

"No, you're not. And then there's that little matter of the Meet Rack."

"I had nothing to do with that."

"You were there."

"Whoever did it must have been planning it

before I got there—"

"Don't be an idiot. It doesn't take that long to plant a bomb. And finally—you spent the night in bed with a Silver."

"He's not a Silver. Not yet. Maybe not ever."

"Close enough for government work. Did he get what he wanted? Did you get what you wanted? Is anybody in this goddamn wasteland getting anything they want?"

I shook my head. "I, um—never mind."

She took a deep breath. "I shouldn't ask, I have no right to, but um—?"

I knew what she meant. I nodded, the barest possible nod.

"I suppose I should congratulate you. Maybe you're getting past it, but probably not." Mom took a deep breath. "For the safety of the city, I should lock you up, but the Silvers would have you out within an hour. It's not worth the trouble."

"The Silvers? Why?"

"How the hell should I know? But someone up there wants you out in the world, stumbling around and destroying things like a minor-league kaiju." She took another heavy breath. I wondered if I should start worrying about her health, but no, she was just recharging her frustration. "Is there anything else you want to tell me? Is there anything else you're planning to destroy?"

Shook my head.

"I'll ask it a different way. You're not done yet, are you? Do I get a warning?"

I thought about telling her. I thought about not telling her.

I thought too long, because she said. "I can't stop you, can I?"

Shook my head again.

She sighed. Right.

"All right," she said. She did something and her desk cleared and shut down. She pulled out a pen and a pad of paper. Very old-fashioned. She scribbled something on the top sheet, shook her head, crumpled it up, then tossed it to me. "Never mind," she said. "Life's too short for this shit. Try and stay out of trouble. Pretend you can do that for me."

Out on the street again. The day was coming up bright and cloudless, revealing the brown ugliness of the parts of the city that still hadn't been rebuilt, and probably never would be.

A car was waiting at the curb. One of *theirs.*

There are no secrets. All you need is an access to the nano-smog.

One day everyone would have it.

Who knew what that would unleash?

What the hell, I got into the car.

I hadn't come this way before. The route passed the remains of what had once been a fabled estate, a monument to wasted wealth. Only the bones of it were left now. It might have been elegant once, but I'd never seen it that way. It had been collapsing into ruin since before I was born. Eventually it would lose the last of its shape and become just another pile of unrecognizable debris.

Nobody would care. The city had more than its share of monuments to the disaster.

The car turned inland then, curving up through young forest, heading eastward toward the land of private canyons and ancient mysteries.

There are gates and there are gates. The ones at the base of the hill are deceptively polite. Just inside is a small parking area. There's no direct road. If a Silver is willing to talk to you—unlikely in any case—a shuttle will come down a narrow track and pick you up. Or you can wait until you give up or die of hunger or thirst.

I know there's a road—the limo took me directly. But only the limo knows where that road is. It doesn't show up on any map, and I'm pretty sure it doesn't exist if you don't know where it is.

My car parked itself. I reached for a water bottle. The shuttle was already waiting for me. Well, they had to know I was coming, the moment my car turned inland.

The little shuttle car was comfortably upholstered. The ride was smooth. The track curved left and right, ducked around some trees, and into a tunnel that corkscrewed up and around, not only confusing my own sense of direction, but probably any tracking devices that I might have been carrying. Eventually, it arrived at a rustic-looking platform.

Stepping down, I was in another garden, this one wilder and unmanicured. It looked like a clearing in a forest—because it was a clearing in a forest.

Red was standing beside the inevitable table —chairs, a pitcher of water, and two glasses.

"Are you thirsty?" he offered.

"I wouldn't say no."

He poured. "Laz tells me you had an interesting evening."

I nodded politely. "Interesting as in pleasant? Or interesting as in dangerous?"

"Both, I expect."

He gestured me to a chair. I sat. He sat opposite.

"You have questions."

"Let's start with the big one. If I asked for the transformation, would you give it to me?"

"Now?"

"Yes, now. If I asked now."

Red smiled. "But you're not really asking. You said 'if.' So any answer I might give you would be irrelevant. But when you're ready to ask me in all seriousness, I'll give you a serious answer."

"Fair enough."

Red sipped his water and waited.

I was never going to ask for transformation. We both knew that. It was just a place to start. A test.

I drank from my own glass. The water wasn't carbonated, but somehow it sparkled. I wondered what they had done to it—or if I was really so physically drained that even ordinary water was a surprise. I put the glass down and said, "Tell me how the Silver was killed."

"Why do you need to know?"

"I'm not a decoy anymore. I'm the real thing."

"An assumption on your part . . ."

"A dead body in my bathtub? An angry tunnel troll? A bomb at the Meet Rack? Did I leave anything out? You might not be taking me serious, but somebody is."

"Yes, that's the point."

"Well then, I'm getting serious too."

Red leaned back in his chair as if he was considering my words. He wasn't. He had already made up his mind. We both knew that too. He had made up his mind even before I'd made up mine to ask. He steepled his hands in front of him, tapping the ends of his fingers to his lips—almost as if praying. Except, as far as I knew, Silvers didn't pray to anyone or anything except themselves.

"We're playing chess," he said. "Mega-chess. The queen does not explain herself to the pawns."

"Is that all I am? A pawn."

"You don't want to be anything more, do you?"

"No. What I want is to get out of the game. It's not my game, it's yours. But that's not possible anymore, is it?"

"Probably not," he admitted. "We needed a distraction. You've certainly provided one."

"So, you owe me."

"From your perspective, yes. From ours—from mine? No."

"I don't want to play word games. Not with you. Not with Laz—although I will admit, playing with Laz, there are two winners. At least I want to think so. Whatever he is, he's the most honest person I've met since any of this began. Or at least, his performance of honesty is the most convincing. You're using him. He's using you. Everybody's getting used—and over here, I'm used up."

"And your point is?"

"I need to know the rest of it."

"No, you don't *need* to know. You *want* to know."

He was right. I didn't have an answer for that. I picked up my glass of water and drank, hoping that something would occur to me. But before it did, Red spoke.

"The question, the *real* question, is whether or not it is useful for you to know. Useful for us, not useful for you."

"And—?"

"I haven't decided. The problem with this decision is that it is asymmetrical. If I tell you nothing, and if it's the wrong decision, I can rectify that. I will always have the option of telling you something in the future. But if I tell you something now, I am stuck with that decision. I can't untell you. So, the real choice for me is whether I want to deal with the consequences now or later. Not just the foreseeable consequences, but the unintended

ones as well. There are always unintended consequences. Too often, they are not only unintended,
they are also unpredictable." He studied me. "Did
you follow that?"

"There's a point you didn't mention," I said.
"There are also consequences, intended, unintended, and unpredictable, for choices you don't
make. So, a choice to postpone a choice is also a
choice."

"Of course. Did you think I was unaware of
that?"

"Of course not. I assume you know what I'm
going to say before I say it. I assume you have already played both sides of the conversation in your
head before even deciding to have it."

"If that's true, then why are we talking?"

"Because you're waiting to see how much
I've figured out."

"Well, yes—you've figured out that much."

"Not that hard. There've been volumes written about Silver psychology. Whole libraries."

"And you've read them all?"

"Enough to know why I won't take the shine.
I don't want to be like you. I don't want to think
like you. It's frustrating."

"Not from this side. From this side, it's occasionally interesting, mostly amusing. Mostly boring. Like when you read a story to a toddler."

"I don't spend much time with toddlers,
they smell funny—and I find the comparison in-
sulting." I realized I was still holding my glass. I

put it down, empty. "You still haven't answered my question."

Red shrugged. "It's too late for the pebbles to vote. The avalanche has already started."

"Tell me something I don't know."

"There are no kings on the board. Only queens."

"That's it?"

Red shrugged. "If you're as smart as you pretend to be, it should be enough."

I didn't answer. I considered.

No kings. Only queens. "Okay. So somebody killed a Silver. They were taking a queen off the board. I got that."

"Keep going."

"How'd they kill her?"

"Irrelevant."

"No. Very relevant."

"Why?"

"Because Silvers can't be killed."

"Yes, that's what people believe."

"Obviously, it isn't true."

Red nodded. "Humans die because the human body isn't designed to withstand injury. The human body is messy. Poke a hole in a human, he bleeds. If he bleeds enough, he dies. If there's internal damage, if it's severe enough, he bleeds inside, his organs shut down—and he dies. Even if you sew up the damage, he can still get infected, and if it's bad enough, he dies. The only thing keeping most humans alive is the desperation of medical science. And even that isn't enough to stop a human body from dying eventually—if not sooner, than later. After how many centuries of medical advancement, the best that humans can do is argue with entropy. But you still can't defeat it."

"But Silvers can?"

"So far—we seem to be immortal. We don't age, unless we choose to. Poke a hole in a Silver and the hole self-seals, no blood. If the hole is deep enough, if the damage is severe enough—the organs go to sleep, the blood self-seals. The body doesn't repair, it rebuilds."

I nodded.

"The human body requires an inordinate amount of energy to maintain itself—healing requires even more energy, because the body not only has to maintain, it also has to invest in repair. But with a Silver, the body slows down, not quite to zero, but slow enough, and available energy is applied to a slow careful reconstruction of the damage. It looks like death, but it isn't. It's one of the things that humans misunderstand about us. We get sick or injured, we go dormant."

"You retire to your coffins."

"We're aware of the symbolism, yes."

"So, does that answer your question how to kill a Silver?"

"You have to destroy the ability of the body to reconstruct—or you have to destroy the body so completely there's not enough to reconstruct . . . ?"

"Precisely." Red waited for me to extrapolate.

"So, a flamethrower would work, wouldn't it? Incinerate the victim."

"That's one way, yes."

"Or a troll could rip the body apart, dismembering it into six or seven pieces . . . ?"

"At least."

"So let me speculate that the Silver in question—a queen in your game—was either killed by a troll or blown up by a bomb or . . . ?"

"The method is irrelevant. What is relevant is that someone was able to get close enough to assassinate."

"Mmm," I said. "That means her—I'm assuming this queen was a her, you will correct me if I'm wrong, but that means her defenses were down. Or breached."

Red smiled. "I'll take it in order. No, I will not correct you if you're wrong. Unless it's useful for me to do so. And there are no defenses against a determined assassin, there are only ways to make the job harder, or impractical, or improbable. One way is to keep oneself secure inside a sanctuary. High walls. Distance. Various security devices. Hiding in a cave or a tunnel so that your assassin can't target you from the sky. Disguising yourself. Faking your death so that you no longer have an official existence—all of those have been tried. And some of them have even been effective. So far.

"There's another way to avoid assassins. Be unpredictable. Change your pattern of behavior every day. Never travel the same route twice, never go to the same place twice. Never wear the same clothes twice. Never be identifiable. Leave early one day, late the next. Have no specific tastes or styles or flavors. Eat sushi today, tacos tomorrow. Change your mannerisms, your gestures, your hair style, your body language, your accent, your cologne, get randomly remodeled. Confuse their targeting. If they're not sure it's you, they might hesitate."

"Does that work?"

"In theory."

"So . . . all these different ways of avoiding assassination—is that your way of telling me that Silvers have some serious enemies?"

"Somebody did kill one."

"At least one," I said. "Are there other deaths you haven't told me about?"

"It's a big board, it's a long game," said Red. "What do you think?"

"I think you're not going to tell me."

"That's right, I'm not." He offered the pitcher. "Do you want some more water?"

I considered my empty glass. I picked it up, jiggled it, put it back down. "No thanks."

FIFTEEN

The ride home was uneventful.

If there were assassins after me, today was not their day. Or I was being unpredictable.

I didn't feel like moving out to the desert—and hiding in a cave or a tunnel wasn't much of an option either.

But there was another way that Red hadn't mentioned, don't be the biggest target. Be unimportant.

That had been my way.

Until *she* invited me into her limo.

And me, thinking I was being smart, got in.

All this thinking, my head was starting to hurt. Again.

There're no kings, only queens.

Maybe I should have figured it out while Red was speaking. Either he wanted me to or he didn't want me to. It didn't matter. Even if I could figure it out, it wasn't going to make sense. Not to me.

Not to any small. And while part of me needed to understand, most of me didn't want to pay the price for an answer that I probably wouldn't like anyway.

I think too much.

Had the car drop me off at the beach. Went to the counter at Mickey's and picked up a stale sandwich and a warm soda. Found a gazebo overlooking the rainbow sand. Ate slowly, tried to look boring. Stood up. Stretched. Tossed the trash in a bin. Wandered down to where the waves splashed harmlessly against the rocks. Stretched. Sighed. Pulled off my coat. Brushed invisible lint away. Looked in the pockets for something. Didn't find it. Found a crumpled note. Made to toss it into the water. No, wait. Uncrumpled it. An address and a time. Crumpled the paper again and tossed it into the water where it disappeared. Did some more useless stuff, brushed more dirt off my clothes, took off my shoes, wandered barefoot back to the grass. Pretended to shake sand out of my shoes, put them on. Wandered in the general direction of the beach house.

Maybe I'd been convincing. Probably not. But might as well go through the motions, just in case.

Set an alarm and fell into bed.

Woke up before the alarm went off. Probably another small tremor, unnoticeable until something rattles in the kitchen. Showered, put on clean underwear, armor and chain mail, long sleeves, leggings, neck brace, helmet, boots, gloves, and a flowing black wrap to cover it all. Super-black cloak with hood. Goggles. The whole enchilada.

Armaments?

Of course.

Opened the floorboards, went downstairs, and wasn't surprised to find that somebody had already been here. They'd restocked the armory. How thoughtful. Some interesting additions.

But I only took what I was certain I would need for personal defense. Not wise to travel through the city armed for tunnel trolls. Too much attention.

Walked two blocks to the metro, took the train downtown, transferred east and got off at the third stop. Half a block west. A rundown-looking warehouse. Nice camouflage.

Inside . . .

Laz met me in the lobby. Escorted me inside.

I'd known places like this existed before the war. I wasn't surprised that this one was still operative. Lots of money was spent here because lots more was at risk. Maintaining it . . . makes sense.

Big. White. Bright. Clean. Industrial. Military-grade shielding. Whoever had originally designed and built this place—they meant business.

It was too bright. Too clean. I felt dirty and out of place.

Turned to Laz. "What are you doing here?"

"Observer," he said.

"For who?"

"Yes."

"Right. I should have known. Okay, lead me."

Conference room. Oversized. Large screens at one end. At the opposite end—Trent. And a heavily armored team. Twenty halflings in black armor and helmets—and three halfling Queens beside them, nine feet tall and almost as wide. And mean looking. Dressed in red, long black hair pulled tight into a bun on top of their heads. They could have been triplets. In my mind, I named them Mary, Victoria, and Elizabeth, but I couldn't really tell them apart. Also a pair of Silvers, but without weapons. I didn't know them. All of them were heavily armored, their helmets glittered with interference shields. The halfling team carried enough weaponry to overthrow a small government.

"Uh-huh," I said. I looked to Trent. "I thought you were dead."

"I thought you were."

"Not this time."

Mom came grunting in, dressed the same. "Skip the introductions," she said, facing me. "You're here as a courtesy—to keep you from getting in the way and screwing things up even more. Follow instructions. Keep out of the way. Whatever you see, you didn't see it. Understand? This place doesn't exist. This operation doesn't exist. You don't exist. I don't exist. None of these people exist. And this place has nano-scrubbers. If you start to feel itchy, that's why. Any questions? Keep them to yourself." She looked me up and down. "Not good enough." She waved to one of the Queens. "Do you have armor that'll fit this one?"

The Queen stumped forward, looked me up and down, nodded. "Strip," she commanded.

I stripped. Completely. Dropped everything on the floor. Straightened up and a hundred pounds of gear was shoved into my arms. When I was dressed again, this time in military grade, Mom gave me a cursory approval, then turned to the others. "Right. Let's roll."

"No briefing?" I asked.

"We had it before you got here. You're irrelevant, remember?"

Somebody shoved a dazzler-equipped flamethrower into my arms. "Do you know how to use this?" I nodded. "Well, don't. Unless you're told to." And we were off.

Six black vans rolled out of the warehouse and rolled silently through empty streets. Supposedly invisible, but even a moving hole is noticeable.

I was in the third one, with Mom. She didn't talk and neither did I.

We didn't go far, only to an abandoned transit station. Trent cut the bolts on the metal gate and two of the Queens led the way down, Mary and Elizabeth, I assumed. Half the team followed. Then the Silvers, Laz, Mom, me, and Victoria, the third Queen, with the rest of the team.

I'd known about the Queens, anyone who

pays attention knows that the halflings have Queens, but I'd never met one before, and I'd never seen one in action, let alone three in one place. I knew only what most people knew. No one becomes a halfling unless a Queen approves and they're very picky, almost as bad as the Silverlights. Halflings were small and slender, but if the rumors were true, they were stronger than bears. If this effort required three Queens and twenty halflings, it wasn't just serious, it was somewhere on the other side of crisis.

Beneath the transit tunnels, service and maintenance tubes. Beneath those, construction shafts. And those led down and down to the hardened burrows where everyone who couldn't flee the city during the war had hid out—well, those who were important enough to be invited.

None of the elevators worked. The escalators were out of service too, we had to walk. We proceeded slowly with the team checking every branching passage, every sideways access, probing everything with beams intense as day.

The sounds of our boots felt unnaturally loud in the deep silence of the earth—and the air felt sweaty down here, unnaturally warm, not a good sign. The lead Queen raised a hand, called a halt, passed the word back in whispers. A nest. Maybe two or three trolls.

She motioned again and the halflings at the front of the team moved forward slowly, every step carefully placed.

A pause. Silence.

We waited in stillness.

Listening.

And then, finally, we could hear it.

A hint of sound.

Very faint and far away.

Like the surf, slowly crashing against the rainbow sands. A slow rising and falling, distant inhalation and exhalation, the breathing of something very large and powerful.

Asleep? Dormant?

The Silvers shook their heads.

No. Not—

Abruptly, a crashing roar—

AND BRIGHTNESS!

The dazzlers blazed, shrieking with light!

Three dark shapes, stumbling, crushing over each other, flailing forward—

The halflings fired.

Even with the earcups, the noise was impossible, echoing and reechoing off the sides of the tunnel. The torches fired, the backwash of heat and light hit us like a wall of pain, forcing all of us backward in hasty retreat.

But ahead—the tunnel trolls were burning. The missiles had penetrated their thick skins, burrowed deep into their bellies, exploding into unquenchable fire. They were burning inside, writhing, screaming, roaring in agony as they died in horror.

It took a long time, long enough to alert

whatever else was down here. Something had happened. Something was coming. If there were more of them down here, they wouldn't retreat, they didn't know how. This was only a beginning.

We couldn't pass the bodies, they blocked the passage. But the Queens referred to the maps on their wrist displays. We backtracked to a side tunnel, followed it to another access and headed downward again. The Queens were resolute. The halflings were determined. The Silvers were dispassionate. I glanced to Laz. He was unreadable.

I didn't know what I felt.

I was just glad I hadn't attempted this on my own.

I thought about Troll Town. Did they feel any kinship with their underground cousins? What we were doing down here was dangerous, not just in the immediate sense. What if they considered these attacks as an act of war?

The human race, in all its varied forms, had barely survived the last one.

By human standards, trolls are stupid. They don't think deep. They don't timebind. They exist in the present, they flicker from one moment of now to the next. They have only the most rudimentary sense of time.

Maybe they would be so exhausted, so overwhelmed and decimated by their own physical excesses that maybe after a few weeks of dormancy to recover their ability to function—maybe these deaths would be so detached from their own ex-

periences, they might not consider them important. Certainly not important enough to distract
from the arrival of huge truckloads of potatoes
and coal and carrots. Maybe a few loads of chocolate too. Unsweetened please.

Timing. Everything was timing. Mom knew
what the danger was. The Silvers did too.

I followed.

I knew why Mom wanted me along—so she
could keep an eye on me, keep me from getting
in the way—but I was beginning to wonder if she
might have another motive as well.

SIXTEEN

We continued downward.

We passed the last level of bunkers. From here down, the passages were rough-hewn as if carved out by giant claws. Well, they had been. We were now entering an unknown realm, places that even the Queens hadn't mapped. So we stopped.

Queens Mary and Elizabeth moved to the lead. One dug into the backpack the other was wearing, pulled out a flat metal box, unfolded it like a book. Almost immediately a flickering cloud of sparkling dust rose from the case and thinned out, swirling ahead, disappearing into the distance. Nano-drones. They'd create a web of awareness, each one flashing its own separate bits of data back to the server where they would be collated into a detailed three-dimensional map.

We weren't going into this blind.

At last, Mary and Elizabeth were satisfied and waved us forward. Downward. Deeper. The beams widened, flooded the passage with light, sometimes narrowing to probe a crevice or side-channel.

It was hotter here. I didn't know about the others, but I was getting uncomfortable under the armor. I had to turn on the cooling. And the smells were worse. I gave up. I pulled my breather into place. I lowered the faceplate on my helmet too. I wasn't the only one.

The nano-drones didn't just map the tunnels, they also located anything that might be lurking below.

We found two nestlings and a guardian in the bottom most wallow. I suppose I should have felt bad about their deaths, but I'd had too many bad experiences with adult trolls. And the young ones weren't cute enough to inspire much pity. I glanced to the Silvers, they were visibly upset, almost shaking. They turned their backs to the carnage and went into that deliberate meditative state that sometimes looked like a vertical coma. I'd heard it could go on for days. I wondered if we'd have to leave them here or drag them along —but no, even as I watched they came aware again. I might have wondered why they were even here, but it was obvious. They needed to be observers and Mom and the Queens needed their input. Their advice? Context. Whatever.

I do know my limits. I'm irrelevant. Keep out of the way and don't screw things up. I was ballast. A decoy. A distraction. An annoying nuisance.

Sand in the gears. Along for the ride so they could keep an eye on me. Whatever. I'd already been paid. I could retire to what was left of Hawaii. But the dead boy in my bathtub, his head in my refrigerator—I wanted payback.

No, I *needed* payback. I needed to wrap my hands around the throat or throats of whoever was responsible for that atrocity, and all the others as well, squeezing the last desperate breath out of them, making them suffer at least as much as all of their victims. Or more. As much as I could manage.

No, I'm not enlightened. I don't even pretend to be. Maybe that's the real reason I won't go Silver. I don't want to be enlightened, Silver or any other color. I don't want to give up revenge.

The nestling trolls died writhing. So did the mother-guard. The stench was incredible.

We should have been done there, but we weren't. We backed up into a side chamber that we could defend if necessary and had a meeting.

There should have been more trolls here. We'd brought more than enough firepower to take out a whole colony. So where were the rest? Mom suggested, maybe they had retreated, probably out to the desert, maybe further, there were tunnels and trolls aren't known for their courage. Maybe they'd panicked when I killed little Beowulf and his mom. Or maybe they'd fled just now, when they realized our advance was unstoppable. Based on the smell, it could have been either. Troll smell doesn't fade with time. It sits in the air like a stubborn fog, only worse. Sunlight can evaporate fog. Wind can push it away. But troll stink just lingers forever. There are theories that it's not just a physical phenomenon but a morphological one as well, but that just explains it. It doesn't solve it.

We kept our masks on.

Well, except the Silvers. I don't know how they did it.

They studied their own map display for a brief moment. Whatever they saw, it was obvious only to them. One of them tapped the screen. "They fled because they were terrified."

Mom replied. "Yes, that's what we said."

"No," said the Silver. "You assumed they were afraid of you. They were not. Trolls have contempt for humans. They respect that human weapons can be painful, sometimes even deadly, but that's why they are contemptuous. Humans need weapons to be strong. Halflings too. Trolls do not. They fled its wrath. Or its hunger."

Queens Mary and Elizabeth nodded.

Mom looked skeptical. "It?"

I nodded. "Yep."

Mom turned to me. "What?"

"Look. There's a hole at the bottom of the map, some place where the nano-drones should have reported back, but didn't. Something stopped them, neutralized them as fast as they arrived."

She looked annoyed. "It looks like a dead end."

"We need to see."

She started to say something about how it would be a stupid waste of time, then stopped herself.

Both of the Silvers were nodding.

SEVENTEEN

So **Mom didn't know everything.** That was interesting too. I wondered what else she might not know.

Very quietly, Laz came up beside me. "You know what's down there, don't you?"

I shook my head.

"You were in the war."

I shook my head again. Not a denial, just a warning. I didn't want to talk about it.

But Laz was persistent. "How old are you, Mandy?"

Maybe I owed him something. Maybe I wanted something too. I said, "Old enough. Cut me in half and count the rings."

"So you have been remodeled." An accusation.

"Rejuved," I said. "Only the body, not the mind."

"Interesting," he said. "So you're not suicidal."

"Not yet. What about you?"

"Thirty-four."

Looked at him. Looked closely. "You're just a kid. I would have guessed more. I have things in the fridge older than you."

He shrugged, unembarrassed. "So if you know what's down there—okay, if you think you know what's down there, and if it's as bad as you think, why aren't you running for the exit?"

"Well," I shrugged. "I might be wrong. Maybe the only thing down there is the granddaddy of all troll farts. Even trolls don't like their own stink."

Laz snorted.

"Yeah. I don't think so either. I want to see for myself. If I'm right, maybe I'll be lucky enough to survive. I've been lucky so far. Why are you here?"

"I'm being paid."

"Yeah, okay." Another thought occurred to me. "If Red offers you the shine, will you take it?"

He nodded.

"Even if it reveals your employer?"

"Red already knows who's paying me. I don't, but he does. That's why he feeds me false information. Whoever is paying me knows that too. Yes, it's a charade. But I'm getting paid and I might get the shine. So . . ." he shrugged. "Why not?"

The Queens finished their conference with Mom and the Silvers. They nodded in agreement and we formed up and moved out.

We moved slowly, cautiously. The footing

was uneven. The passage was rough and jagged as if it had been chewed out of the rock by something very large, something that didn't care much about neatness, only about getting where it was going. We picked our way through flickering darkness, the dazzle-beams shifting and revealing the broken surfaces all around us. Something big had forced its way through here. We followed down through the proof its passage, a jagged tube spiraling deep into darkness and uncertainty.

Every step was more difficult than the last. The temperature was unnaturally high. It was hot enough here that the cooling engines of our armor couldn't keep up. I was sweating, sipping at my water tube only when the monitor allowed.

And the stink—our masks were good, but the stink still came through. What it would be like without our breathers, I didn't want to know. I wasn't going to test it.

We all had to watch our footing carefully, sometimes helping each other cross a bit of difficult terrain. The halflings taking the point flashed their dazzle-beams ahead, up and down as well. The jagged walls of the tunnel were illuminated with alternating shards of brightness and shadows that shifted with the beams. We had to take it one step at a time, the footing was uncertain. The broken rocks might shift and slide beneath our weight. As careful as we were, our boots still crunched across the uneven surface. In the deep silence of the tunnel, every scrape, every rattle of loose gravel—it felt too loud. Who or what might be listening ahead. Behind every downward curve lurked an unknown potential. The map said there was nothing there.

But neither was there anything in the darkness when I turned my bedroom lights out. I still sleep with a night light.

We went deeper into the heat and the stink and the darkness—

—Until Queens Mary and Elizabeth stopped us, long enough to listen, long enough to study their map again. Finally, they pointed ahead, motioning us forward. There was no chatter. Nothing. Only the rustle of our passage, the soft crunch of our boots. No one spoke. If any of the others suspected what might lie ahead of us, none of them said anything. Halflings don't talk much to outsiders anyway. They say we don't understand and they're probably right, but halflings have a reputation for being ferocious in battle. That's probably what Mom was depending on.

The deeper we went, the more I was certain. This dark tunnel couldn't be anything but the proof of something that shouldn't be here, shouldn't even exist at all.

We came to an edge—

EIGHTEEN

—a**nd stopped.**

Before us, beneath us—a cavern, a crater, a huge stinking wallow carved out of the earth by something large and deadly. Even with the rebreathers, the smell was overwhelming. It turned its massive head around and studied us dispassionately.

A nesting fury.

These things were supposed to be extinct.

It blinked wetly. Its eyes oozed with something like mucus, only green and toxic. It opened its cavernous mouth and hissed, a long blast of heat and stink. A threat.

Furies don't rear up, they lift themselves slowly, a mountain of black scales, a laborious fleshquake. It pulls thick legs beneath its bloated body and rises like a tidal wave, dreadful and unstoppable. It towers.

To their credit, the Queens were equally formidable. I didn't hear the command, the fury roared, sudden smoke and flame, the rockets—ten, twelve, more!—flashed and struck. Some bounced off its armored body, but others penetrated deep, burrowing into the vulnerable underbelly of the beast where they detonated, each one a blast of liquid oxygen, expanding into boulders of frozen tissue, momentarily hardening until the heat of the creature's own body liquified the gas—and then the waiting detonators went off, igniting the gas pockets inside, flashing fires exploded within, shuddering the beast, rolling it back on its stout hind legs.

The halflings fired again, another dozen rockets, and another dozen after that. The fury shrieked and gurgled and thrashed—it writhed until it died, but even then its body still shuddered in a desperate settling toward a final equilibrium, fleshquakes rippled outward from its devastated center.

Smoke. Stench. Heat. Bubbling noises. A last gurgle in its throat. A long last exhalation from the collapsing organs that served as lungs. But finally, stillness.

The halflings were pros. They didn't lower their weapons. They waited. Furies never died easily. And sometimes they somehow rechannel their multiple inner biologies and come back to life unexpectedly. Always a surprise to those who think they've triumphed. Furies can be patient, taking months to rebuild their internal organs and eventually coming back stronger than ever. A near perfect war weapon.

One of the Queens turned to Mom, maybe Elizabeth. "I can't give you certainty. And I'm not sending anyone down there to implant bio-probes. We'll plant seismic detectors up here instead. Any tremor—we'll return and repeat. As many times as necessary. And it will be necessary."

Queen Mary pointed. "This is a nest. And that's a mother. And she's got a clutch of at least seven eggs beneath her. They'll hatch, maybe they already have. No way to know. No safe way, that is. They'll feast on her belly fat for a year or more. Dead or alive, they won't care. If she's alive, neither will she. She won't even notice for a year or two. But if she's dead, not likely, but if she is—that's another problem. Because the younglings will keep eating until there's nothing left of the body. After that, unpredictable. They might feed on each other until there's only one left. Or, if they're disturbed before then, if there are multipole survivors and they're disturbed, they'll go into rage-mode—and we'll have a real problem."

Mom nodded.

And then Queen Elizabeth looked up from her scanner. "This mother died too easily. She was weak. If her eggs have already hatched, if there are younglings, if they've been feeding on her, then the problem is already here."

The ground shuddered. Not a lot. But enough that we all looked to each other. And then it shuddered again. This time worse—

187

There was more than one.

They came roaring up from below, an eruption of rage, boiling over the edge in an upward avalanche of teeth and claws and fury—

NINETEEN

Dreams that glimmered and then receded.
Floating.
I opened my eyes to silver light.
She was there.
I closed my eyes.

She put a straw in my mouth. I sipped cool water. An eternity of relief. When I'd had enough, she put it away. I wondered if I could clear my throat.

"Don't try to talk," she said. "You're in recovery. You were pretty badly broken, it'll take time but you're going to be all right." I felt her hand on mine. I didn't have the strength to pull it away. I wasn't sure I wanted to. "You've been asleep for a while, Mandy. Most of a year. A lot has happened."

She paused. "You're still on maintenance. You're not going to feel anything for a while. So maybe this is the best time to tell you. A lot has happened." She squeezed my hand. "There were three of them. Half-grown. They couldn't be stopped. Mom was killed in the attack. So were two of the Queens. And seven of the halflings. They were finally driven back by the surviving halflings. Laz pulled you out, he carried you most of the way."

She fell silent then, waiting. Mom dead. Queens dead. Halflings dead. Furies still under the city. And I'm—feeling weird.

"The trolls blamed the furies. A hundred of them, maybe more, went down into the tunnels. It was bad. The whole city shook for a day. There were places where the ground opened up, there were terrible sounds and smells. Were they killed? Or did something else happen? Something worse? Nobody knows. Whatever happened down there, none of them ever came back. Everything is collapsed, impassible. There haven't been any quakes, so we think the furies were neutralized, but we have no way of knowing for sure. And yes, we are working on it. We have to be certain. But it'll be years. Nobody knows what to plan for. It's not your problem anymore. All of that—it happened more than a year ago."

I opened my eyes and looked at her. I didn't care. She looked the same, but different. Deeper. I closed my eyes again.

She must have noticed. She pressed her hand on mine. "It's taken a long time to restore you, but listen to me. You're going to be all right. But your body—there was only one way to save you. It was necessary. In time, you'll understand."

She did something I couldn't sense and I disappeared again for a while. This time the glimmers were stronger. I felt something out there, an awareness. Then I faded away.

Each time I drifted back, the feelings were more distinct.

Until—

The day.

I opened my eyes and looked at my hand.

I was shining.

I was expanding. Awakening.

I felt it all.

I listened and I could hear the multitudes —all the minute whispers of the nano-smog that swirled around and through me, inside and out, everywhere and everything and everyone, all at once. I could see inside myself and out beyond as well. I could hear the music of the world. I could smell and taste and feel it all—the groaning of whales in the deep, the chittering of insects in the sky, the susurrus of the wind as it wrapped around the mountains, the unhappy sliding of massive seas as the moon pulled them back and forth, the slow turning of the globe as its hemispheres shifted out of one season and into the next. I could disappear into the sea of souls. I could feel their hearts beating, their lungs expanding with each breath, their muscles sliding and stretching. It was too much, too much—

But I couldn't stop. I stretched outward, ever outward, trapped in the fascinations of experience.

I drifted like flotsam, the tsunami of sensation swept through me and I was carried along with it—

Until I shut it out. Shut it off.

Because a part of me, a lonely distant part, a screaming remnant of the past, a last bit of who I used to be, raged, raged against the glory of the shine.

I understood the emotion. It was real. And it was trapped like an insect in amber inside the expanded newness of me.

Despite all the times that I'd said no, they'd done it anyway.

They'd known. All of it. Everything. How could they not?

I'd hated them for knowing how much I wanted it.

And then I'd hated myself for wanting it.

So I couldn't ever say it. Couldn't let them be right. Couldn't let anyone.

That last little part of me, the one that had retreated—it still retreated now, retreated deep inside of me, festering and screaming and clawing at the walls of its self-created emotional cage, and I wondered, was it like this for all of them? For every Silverlight?

Did the past need to be caged until it could be finally, desperately, exonerated? Assimilated? Owned.

I resumed breathing. I concentrated on

breathing. In, out, again. I concentrated on dis-covering my body, my feet and legs and thighs, my groin and belly, chest and arms and hands, my neck and face, my eyes and ears and tongue and nose—

I am Silver now. Like it or not.

I kinda liked it.

But—

Now I was becoming aware.

I think and I know things.

TWENTY

Outside, the gardens sang to me. The leaves whispered of the air, the wind told stories of the city. The trees stretched slowly toward the sky. The ground mumbled in its sleep, worms slipped through the earth. Insects slept in their cocoons, struggled out, fed and bred and died in the mandibles and beaks of others.

Sitting and listening to it all, listening to the world below, the distant sounds of auto engines, tires on asphalt, brakes squealing, sirens like metal banshees, heavy doors opening and closing, sudden thunks, cries of pain and surprise, an occasional bang and clang.

And the smells, all the smells—the aromas of the kitchens and the dumpsters and the machines, all mixed together in a cacophony of flavors, all the spices of the city in a churning stew of humans rushing about, like little organic machines, traveling back and forth on rails of channeled behavior.

The nano-smog brought me sounds and savors, musical notes and a chorus of muttering data, desperately trying to sort itself into information. Assimilation was a skill. I'd have to practice it, but there was so much out there, so much to see and hear and taste and ultimately to know.

I was lost in wonder.

And the question. Always the question. Unanswerable.

I am what I have become.

Whatever I was before, I am not that anymore. Whatever I am now, that's who I am.

What I thought then and what I think now —all of it, that endless internal conversation, all of it is irrelevant. All that time, the vast investment of feeling, it meant nothing then and means nothing now.

There is only existence. There is only awareness and everything that comes with it. Experience. Choices. A multitude of responsibilities.

Silver meditation. Only a few seconds. And I am *in the state.*

Dispassionate amazement.

Open my eyes and Red is sitting opposite me.

He doesn't need to speak. Neither do I. So we sit for a while.

Finally.

"You understand?"

"She asked you to save me."

"Yes. Conditionally."

I took a drink of water. Waited for him to answer the unasked question.

"You could refuse the shine."

"And die?"

"Yes. That's the same choice all of us have."

"Have others taken it?"

"A few. At the beginning. Before we learned how to tell." His look was penetrating. "You have a question."

"The same one. Why me?"

"The same answer. Because she wanted you."

"Is that how it works?"

"No. Not always." He smiled. "In fact, rarely. Almost never. Actually, you're the first."

"So why me?"

"Because she wanted you."

"Why?'

"Because that's what she wanted."

"She's that important?"

"We're all important." He looked around, waved a hand to indicate the world below. "All of that down there, you've been listening?"

I nodded. "Listening, tasting, feeling—"

"That's only the beginning. Your senses will only expand. Including your time-sense. No, I won't explain. You'll get it when you get it. That's a long way off. You're still learning how to shine. What you've been experiencing, that's barely the start of what's possible. Eventually, you'll connect. You'll *become*. And then you won't need to ask the question."

I nodded. "Talking to me now—so you're talking to a toddler."

He smiled. "Why do you think Silvers avoid going down there?"

"Because humans—they're trapped inside themselves."

"That's one way of saying it, yes."

"No," I said. "We're trapped inside ourselves." I held up my hands to show him. They sparkled. "All of this—we're still humans. Expanded, yes, but still—and like all of those below, we're still trapped. Only it's a larger trap. Much larger, but still a trap. There's no way out, is there?"

"Very good," he said. "You are right on schedule." He levered himself to his feet, looked at me oddly. "There's something else?"

That's when I killed him.

Silvers can't kill—that's what they want you to believe. But I wasn't completely Silver yet.

And neither was Red.

TWENTY-ONE

The same café. I sat alone.

The place was empty.

People came in, they saw I was there, they turned around and left.

The owners were afraid to ask me to leave. Or maybe they didn't want me to. I paid well for the silence.

She came in. Sat down opposite me.

No need to talk. The silence was louder.

A waiter put coffee in front of her. She ignored it.

"Well," she said finally. "That was interesting."

"Sorry for the mess. But it was the only way to be sure."

"I know."

"Are they going to kill me?"

"Probably not. They're afraid of you. Or maybe they will because they're afraid of you. Hard to say. They're still meditative."

"They won't. They don't want anyone to know that Silvers can kill."

"You weren't completely Silver," she said.

"Neither was Red."

"He hid it well."

"Uh-huh. It's hard to keep a secret from a Silver."

"But not impossible. Let me tell you yours. It's why you're something else." She continued dispassionately. "You had three rejuvenations. The first one you had your bones sintered with polycarbon and you had your nervous system replaced with fiber optics and your musculature plasticized. You also had your lung capacity altered and your tissue storage of oxygen enhanced. Your second rejuvenation enhanced your reaction times with predictive data-processing—and petabyte chips to provide you with additional storage. Your third rejuvenation included a necessary upgrade for enhanced reintegration of all previous systems, plus additional enhancements to your primary and secondary senses. All of that—that was why you survived the furies. An unenhanced human wouldn't have."

"I kind of assumed that."

"None of it was a secret, you know. Not from Red or anyone else who could listen to the nanobots. That was why you were invited to take the shine. We needed to know if your enhancements would be useful to us. That was why it took so long to reintegrate you, to preserve them."

"You said 'We.' You said 'Us.'"

She nodded. "I was never alone. And neither were you. Red was not—"

"I know. I think I knew it from the beginning. He was too confident. He was playing too hard. All those redheaded murders—those poor boys were his clones, created only for one thing. To die. Because he wanted the Silvers to feel threatened. That was his control. Those bodies were just props to him. If I still had human emotions, I'd be outraged."

"We suspected. But none of us had access to the bodies. And the nano-web was insufficient. Blocked perhaps. When did you—"

"Laz," I said. "He was another one. Red was using him too. Laz was never going to get the shine. Red couldn't take the risk of discovery. He expected Laz to be killed by the fury. He didn't realize that his clones were as stubborn as he was. Oh, and Laz's payments from that unnamed source? Those were a decoy. Red paid him through a dummy so he would always know what Laz could know or tell. Red was bored with immortality, so he was playing chess with himself to make things interesting. When things got a little too weird, he decided to remove a couple of annoying pawns from the board. The Meet Rack explosion. That was a lucky moment for Laz and me. Unlucky for Red."

"And the furies?"

"Red knew they were there. He'd arranged

their retreat during the final days of the war. He thought he could control them. He was almost right, just not enough. There are still a lot of furies out there." I looked across at her, met her penetrating gaze. "Did I miss anything?"

She shook her head. "Only a couple details."

"There is one more thing . . ."

She waited.

"I don't need to know. I'm just curious now."

"Say it."

"Did you ever really love me?"

"Did you?"

"I thought I did."

"So did I."

ABOUT THE AUTHOR

 **David Gerrold's work is known around the world.** His novels and stories have been translated into more than a dozen languages. His TV scripts are estimated to have been seen by more than a billion viewers.

Gerrold's prolific output includes stage shows, teleplays, film scripts, educational films, computer software, comic books, more than 50 novels and anthologies, and hundreds of articles, columns, and short stories.

He has worked on a dozen different TV series, including *Star Trek, Land of the Lost, Twilight Zone, Star Trek: The Next Generation, Babylon 5*, and *Sliders.* He is the author of *Star Trek*'s most popular episode "The Trouble With Tribbles."

Many of his novels are classics of the science fiction genre, including *The Man Who Folded Himself,* the ultimate time travel story, and *When HAR-*

LIE Was One, considered one of the most thoughtful tales of artificial intelligence ever written. His stunning novels on ecological invasion, *A Matter For Men, A Day For Damnation, A Rage For Revenge,* and *A Season For Slaughter,* have all been best sellers with a devoted fan following. His young adult series, *The Dingilliad,* traces the healing journey of a troubled family from Earth to a far-flung colony on another world. His *Star Wolf* series of novels about the psychological nature of interstellar war are in development as a television series.

A ten-time Hugo and Nebula award nominee, David Gerrold is also a recipient of the Skylark Award for Excellence in Imaginative Fiction, the Bram Stoker Award for Superior Achievement in Horror, and the Forrest J. Ackerman lifetime achievement award.

In 1995, Gerrold shared the adventure of how he adopted his son in *The Martian Child,* a semi-autobiographical tale of a science fiction writer who adopts a little boy, only to discover he might be a Martian. *The Martian Child* won the science fiction triple crown: the Hugo, the Nebula, and the Locus. It was the basis for the 2007 film *Martian Child* starring John Cusack and Amanda Peet.

Gerrold's greatest writing strengths are generally acknowledged to be his readable prose, his easy wit, his facility with action, the accuracy of his science, and the passions of his characters. An accomplished lecturer and world traveler, he has made appearances all over the United States, England, Europe, Canada, Australia, and New Zealand. His easy-going manner and disarming humor have made him a perennial favorite with audiences.

David Gerrold is the 2022 winner of the Robert A. Heinlein Award.

BOOKS BY DAVID GERROLD

from Starship Sloane Publishing

A lifetime in the Labor Corps—or colonize a new world. For Jamie and José, not much of a choice. But Praxis wouldn't be easy. To survive there, you had to depend on each other. And that requires honesty that few possess. Praxis is a bold experiment in society building, a monosexual colony, with no promises of survival and no return trip. But it's got potential. You just have to build a new civilization—on the other side of the universe.

The Man Without a Planet is a science fiction reimagining of the classic tale, "The Man Without a Country"—Redmonde had found his niche in the glitterships of high society, reveling in the opulence and gamesmanship it afforded, until a sudden regime change leads to his permanent exile in the far reaches of space aboard starships building a network of portals through the cosmos. He will never be allowed to see his home world again and escape would seem to be an impossibility—but when the opportunity presents itself, Redmonde disappears into legend.

Dar is a well-connected arbiter and Turtledome is comfortable enough. But the colony on Praxis requires his expertise in crafting a constitution—and he doesn't really have a choice in the matter. Their objective is a bold one, and if they succeed, powerful interests and a highly lucrative, intergalactic economic system will be disrupted. Permanently. A world is at play, the stakes are high, and a corporate overlord will stop at nothing to protect its investment.

Whatever you do, don't piss off Slither. That's the only warning you're going to get. Slither is an augmented, shapeshifting assassin with a hair-trigger temper. Hurled across space to a world of violence and treachery, a place where no one can be trusted, Slither can't get home until she (or maybe he?) stops an interplanetary invasion. What happens next is a ferocious, fast-paced brawl where revenge is a dish best served NOW. Fasten your seatbelt! This is David Gerrold at his best!

Available everywhere that great books are sold!

FORTHCOMING BOOKS BY DAVID GERROLD

Praxis II: Praxis Makes Permanent

The Praxis Papers (Praxis I & II)

Thank you for purchasing this book.